# I'LL FIND YOU

# I'LL FIND YOU

RICHARD HIMMEL

**CUTTING EDGE**

ISBN-13: 978-1-7344295-7-2

Published by
Cutting Edge Publishing
PO Box 8212
Calabasas, CA 91372

# CHAPTER ONE

In the dream, there was the sound of the doorbell ringing, ringing hard and ringing consistently. I don't remember the dream, I don't remember what I dreamed about. But I remember how the ringing was, the persistence of it, cutting through my head like a high voltage shock, but not quick as a shock is, more constant than that, more penetrating. As I woke up the dream faded but the buzzing kept on. My head was heavy, plenty heavy. It was hard to focus my eyes. The room was a blur, the objects in it fuzzy. The illuminated dial of the electric clock was distorted in shape and I couldn't tell what time it was. I could only feel the heaviness of my head and the heaviness of it being pierced by the sound of the doorbell.

Slowly, I sat up in bed and where the heaviness was, I now felt pain too. I got out of bed carefully, putting my feet on the floor gently, not quite sure that the floor would be there. But it was and I began to feel a little better then. There was a bath towel on the floor. I picked it up and wrapped it around my body and went through the living room to see the bastard who was spending the morning leaning on the doorbell.

There were two men standing in the hall when I opened the door. A tall man, taller than I, and a shorter one with his finger glued to the button. I knocked his arm down, hard, and gave him a push. He didn't show any fight but the other man, the bigger one, brushed me aside with his body and walked into the living room. I slammed the door in the little one's face and walked over to see what the hell was going on. The little guy started in on the buzzer again.

"Tell your boy to stop that," I said, "or he's not going to feel so well for a couple of days."

The big man got up from the couch and opened the door for his buddy and then they both came in and sat down.

"O.K. What's up, what's this about?" I asked.

The big man took a stack of papers from his inside pocket, he cleared off the table in front of the couch, putting two empty bottles and a couple of glasses on the floor. It was Irish whiskey, I should have known it. There's nothing in the world that can leave you with a head like I had except Irish whiskey. He pulled a fountain pen out of his pocket and took his time about unscrewing the cap and getting it set up for writing.

"Your name is John Patrick Maguire?"

"It says so on the doorbell, doesn't it?"

He wrote my name down at the top of a form. "Your address is 6082 Briargate?"

I watched him write some more. "What is your age, Maguire?"

"I asked you what this is about. I'm not giving out any information until I know what's going on here."

He pulled a shield from his pocket which was no surprise to me. "My name is Stanleigh," he said, "and this man's name is Corcoran. We are from the police department." His voice was calm and almost syrupy, unruffled. I don't like guys who sound smooth like that. I didn't like him. There was an expression around his mouth, a mean expression, tight-lipped. And he had a baby-face and watery blue eyes that didn't look as though they belonged to a man over six feet tall and weighing more than two hundred pounds. I had a run-in with someone like that in the Army once. I didn't come out so well. He had the brass over me.

"How old are you, Maguire?"

"Thirty-two."

The little man sat slumped over in a chair, looking around all the time. He hadn't taken off his hat. I would have laid twenty-to-one that he was bald.

"What is your profession, Maguire?"

"I asked you what this was about," I said. "I don't have to answer any questions until I know what this is about."

"It's part of a routine, Mr. Maguire. We are investigating something and we have to ask you some questions. We don't like to have to get up so early in the morning. We don't like to have anything to do with people like you." His eyes were on the empty bottles. I couldn't figure out what kind of a cop it was who turned up his nose at liquor. This Stanleigh was queer from the beginning. "But we have a job to do and we have to do it. Now, is all of this clear to you, Mr. Maguire?"

I did not say anything. I had no idea what they could want and my head was not clear enough to play cat and mouse with them. I needed a cigarette. I asked Stanleigh for one.

He took one from his pack, lighted it himself and then handed it to me. He had gotten it all wet and I felt like ramming it in his face. My head seemed to be clearer after I had taken a few swallows of the smoke. I noticed the little man then, staring through the opened bedroom door. I turned to see what was so interesting.

I had forgotten about Tina. She lay there only partially covered by the sheet, sleeping peacefully, not aware that the beady eyes of the little man were examining her. I went over and closed the door quietly and then I yelled. "What the hell's the matter with your little stooge, Stanleigh? Hasn't he ever seen skin before? Take him on a vice raid sometime and ..."

Stanleigh interrupted me, his voice still calm and patient. "Let's see," he said, "you're a lawyer, aren't you?" He waited for an answer but I didn't say anything. He wrote the word "lawyer" in the proper place. "And you're not married, are you, Maguire?" He said it without cracking a smile or looking toward the bedroom, yet all the time I knew he was having himself a good laugh.

"If you know all the answers, Stanleigh, what do you want with me?"

But nothing bothered him. He went ahead and asked the next question on the form he was filling out.

"Your business address is 36 East State Street?"

So I figured, what the hell. They'd get the answers out of me anyway. It wasn't important. I might as well bide my time and see what this was about.

"Yes," I said, "36 East State Street. Room 702."

"That's the way, Maguire. Now, you're being a good boy."

I sat down in the chair at the far end of the room and waited for the rest of the questions. He asked routine things: where I had been born and how long I had lived in various places—things that didn't make any difference. He wouldn't hurry, this Stanleigh guy. He talked slowly and wrote slowly. His voice never changed. Even when he asked the big question, the question that came out and hit me between the eyes, even then his voice was calm.

"Why did Shirley Wolffner commit suicide?"

At first it didn't make any sense. He said the words and I heard the words but they didn't mean anything to me for a minute. Then, it hit me. Hit hard. I suppose everything there was to say, the expression on my face was saying for me. I don't know if Stanleigh saw it, probably he did in spite of the fact that he seemed to be looking down at that piece of paper all the time. I felt everything go hot inside me. I had to keep my fists clenched to hold myself together. It was that bad.

"When did she do it?" I asked.

"Some time between the time you left her last night and five o'clock this morning when her clothes were found on the beach near her apartment building."

In my mind I was seeing the lake as it had been last night, the way we had seen it together. If I had thought about it, if I had had any suspicion, I would have known that that was the way she would do it. For the lake was outside her window, always beckoning.

I couldn't speak. There was so much I could say and yet there was nothing to say. It was over, just like that. It was all build-up and no climax. I could still feel her body where I had held her against me, the warmth which had been in it and the cold, the intensity of the moment in which I had held her, feeling her lips, the split second of yielding and the promise of more to come. Now, there would be nothing. Nothing at all. Nothing except the ache my muscles still had for her.

Stanleigh must have repeated the question twice be-for I heard him. "What was your relationship to Mrs. Wolffner?"

"Relationship?"

"Yes," he said, "relationship. You know what that means, don't you? Relationship."

"I had no relationship with her and I don't like the way you say it. I knew her, if that's what you mean. I knew her in a business way. Her husband was a client of mine."

"Died recently, didn't he?" Stanleigh was reading from a typewritten report.

"Yes."

"In an automobile accident in Nebraska. Traveled a lot, was the sales manager of a hardware firm." Then Stanleigh smiled for the first time. He had dirty yellow teeth. "Quite a difference in their ages, wasn't there?"

I didn't answer. It was all there for him to read if he wanted to know it.

Wolffner had been a nice guy, probably my only client who was on the up-and-up in a business way. I don't know how he ever got hold of me. I always meant to ask him but I never did. He just showed up at my office one day when I was working a cross-word puzzle. I think maybe he stood downstairs in the lobby of the building and looked over the directory until he found a name that he liked. He had just gotten married then and wanted to make a new will. One thing led to another and pretty soon he was calling me up and asking me questions every week or so. He was a man about fifty-five years old, the kind who had plugged hard all his life and worked his way up. He had made lucky plunges in the market and was worth a sizable bundle plus a lot of insurance. I knew him for over six months before he told me about his wife, that she was thirty-two years younger than he and the sweetest girl in the whole world. It was kind of a funny story about the way he married her. Her father had been the owner of a hardware store in Clayton, Kansas, and Wolffner had been traveling that territory off and on for many years, been a pal of the girl's father. He showed up there once to find that the man had died three weeks before and that this daughter was running the hardware store, making a mess of it, the way Wolffner told it. He stayed and helped her out and, I guess, fell for her hard. At any rate, they were married and he sold the store and they moved back here.

Wolffner wanted to be friendly with me but he was a shy man and didn't know how to do it exactly. He apologized several times for not having me up to his house but promised that as soon as the honeymoon was over he wanted me to meet his wife. He kept telling me that his wife was a little bewildered by living in such a big city and that she hadn't wanted to make any friends as yet. I used to tease him and tell him I hoped that when I was his age I could keep a young girl satisfied like that, keep her so satisfied she didn't want to have anything to do with anyone but me. He blushed and looked pleased as hell.

I didn't care whether I ever met his wife or not. He paid his bills promptly and it was pleasant to have a client who was not trying to keep the government from finding out something about him. Besides, I figured she couldn't be much to get hot over. What could you expect from the hardware queen of Clayton, Kansas?

It wasn't until after Wolffner had been killed that I met her. She called me up and said she wanted to see me. She said that Wolffner had told her that if anything ever happened to him that I was the man who knew all about his affairs. It was a couple of days after the funeral and she sounded as though she had never stopped crying.

I skipped my afternoon soiree at the billiard table and went up there. They lived on the sixteenth floor of a big apartment building overlooking the lake. A maid let me in. Shirley Wolffner was sitting by the window looking out over the lake. It was a grey day and the lake was grey. She was dressed in black and used no make-up.

At first, she didn't look like anything, maybe just a little better than a hardware man's daughter from Kansas. But as I talked to her I began to see things in her. It's funny about plain looking girls, sometimes you wonder why guys marry them. I knew that day, I knew that underneath that plainness she had something, she had something that Wolffner had never touched. He had been gentle with her, he was that kind of man. He had treated her as a doll which might break. She wasn't like that, not inside, not where it counts. She needed some rough stuff, she needed a guy like me to let her have it, to give it to her good.

I don't know how you sense those things about a woman, it certainly isn't anything you can learn in a book. You just know it, that's all. You know it without thinking about it. You know it like Di Maggio knows when to hit the ball. You know it or you don't know it.

I knew that day that this girl was for me, that she was my kind of girl. I knew that she could take a lot of hell and give a lot, that she could make you twist and holler and scream and break furniture and get roaring drunk. And she could make you gentle as a kitten is gentle. I knew it. Everything I had knew it. It was there inside me, a nice hard knot in the pit of my stomach.

Funny, all these things were inside me and I couldn't tell one thing she was thinking. She hardly looked at me. I was only a voice in the room. For her, there was only the grey lake outside and her tears, tears which seemed to come from an endless source. It didn't figure. I couldn't see how a girl like her could be so overboard for old Sam Wolffner.

We talked about his investments and insurance for a while and she seemed to know most of what he had and what he was worth. She told me that she wanted everything converted into cash and that she wanted the cash brought to her at the apartment. I stopped thinking about how good she could be long enough to argue with her and tell her how foolish it was to convert her stocks and bonds. I explained how they were making money for her and all that but it made no impression. She had something in the back of her mind and there was no talking her out of it. Finally, I explained the danger there would be in having all that dough in the apartment, even for a little while. There was a safe in the hall closet, she said, and the money would be all right there.

I tried to talk her out of doing it, I tried hard but it was no use. Finally she cried a lot harder and told me she didn't feel well and asked me to leave.

I didn't see her again for about a week. I spent most of that week thinking about her and wondering what the hell there was about her that had hit me so hard. But it was one of those things that I couldn't get out of my system unless I really got it out of my system, the right way. I wanted her so bad that my whole insides went to hell. I had a week in which the days were filled with dreaming and the nights were filled with hard drinking and hard whoring. The whoring wasn't any good. When it was over, the feeding was still there, not diminished at all. I wanted her that much more.

All the business she wanted me to do could have been done in a week but I had a campaign. I had it all figured out how I was going to play it smart, make her want me. I was going to stall, let her stew a little bit, let her get lonesome. I went up there one night. I had to laugh at myself, the time I took getting dressed before I went over there and consulted her about a lot of decisions I had already made. By converting everything, plus the insurance money, there would be about two hundred thousand dollars in cash. She didn't seem impressed one way or the other.

She still cried that night when I talked to her. She told me about her husband, how much she had loved him, what a fine man he had been and how untimely his death was. I tried to find the loophole, I kept searching for the phony ring in her story. It didn't add up. She couldn't have been so nuts for the guy that life wasn't worth living anymore. There was too much blood in her for that—too much good, hot blood.

But there was nothing, no loopholes.

I had to sit tight with this wanting for her inside me, burning harder and harder. I had to play the role of the old family retainer, good old Uncle Johnny, always so consoling when something happens. I was playing it smart all right, I was winning my way into her confidence. And I was taking my time. That, I figured, was the perfect strategy, taking time.

Then, last night, I delivered the money. It had felt good to hold it in my hand. A couple of times, in the cab going over there, I saw myself in some remote tropical island, sitting in a white suit in a bar drinking absinthe, feeling two hundred thousand dollars in my pocket. It felt good for a minute. Only for a minute. I wanted her more than I wanted that money. For the first time in my life I wanted something more than I wanted money.

There was no change in her that night. She didn't seem excited about getting all the cash and she wasn't concerned about what might happen to it. She put it in a tall safe in the front closet which was meant mainly for fur coats, I guess. There was nothing there when she put the cash in except a set of golf clubs. Pretty good clubs.

I invited myself to have a drink. She wouldn't join me. She went back to looking out the window, I asked her what her plans were, and she said that she had none. I figured maybe she would head back for Kansas making my operation a little difficult, but she said that she couldn't, that she would never go back there. She talked about her father and about the hardware store and a little about her girlhood. All the time I was pouring Wolffner's best brandy down my stomach and it wasn't doing anything to me.

She stopped talking completely then and sat in the chair by the window. I stood near her, looking out on the choppy lake, the great white caps of the waves seeming so very white in the night. The moon was there, clear and cold.

"It's going to get very cold," I said.

She didn't answer.

"You sure you don't want a drink? It'll do you good."

"No."

I walked around the room, holding my drink. She seemed completely engulfed in her own thinking, in her own mood. I wanted her to look at me, I wanted to transmit some of what I was feeling to her. I wanted her to know what was going on inside me. There was a chance it might work. There was a chance that I could make her feel it too.

I raised the cover on the keyboard of the piano and ran my thumb quickly across the keys. She jumped and for a moment her eyes blazed. I don't know what the sound of the piano meant to her. Whatever it meant, the sound of it had let her flash some fire my way.

"Don't do that," she said. "Please, don't."

"Sorry. I didn't mean to frighten you." I pointed to the piano. "You play?"

"A little," she said.

"Would you play for me?"

"No. I don't think I'll ever play again."

Oh, baby, I was thinking, you're going to play a lot of things again. You're going to play a lot of things you never played before.

"Mr. Wolffner used to tell me how you played for him," I said. "He loved to hear you play. I don't think he'd like it if you never played again."

She smiled. "He was so silly about me," she said. "He thought I was the most wonderful pianist in the world. He wanted to bring teachers here from New York. He wanted me to play on the concert stage. He was so foolish."

I didn't have to hear her play to know that she wasn't cut out for the concert stage.

"I don't think he was so foolish," I said. "I'd like to hear you play. Please. Play some of the things that Mr. Wolffner used to like."

She was shy at first, sitting down at the piano quite primly and fidgeting on the bench. As she began to play I walked back to the liquor cabinet and poured myself another glass of brandy and listened to her from there. I don't know anything about music but I know she wasn't any great shakes. She played something classical and light, forced and without feeling. When she had finished she turned around. "That was one of Sam's favorites. He would sit in the chair there by the window and listen to me for hours." She laughed a little. "I guess I have been lucky. I only had him for a short time but I think I had more in that. ... I guess I sound silly."

I moved over to the chair by the window where Sam had sat. She was opening up a little bit and I had to play it more cautiously than ever. It seemed inconceivable to me that the Sam she was talking about was the same man whom I had known. A girl, this girl, couldn't have been really in love with Wolffner. It wasn't any other man, though. It was the same Wolffner. There was his picture on the radio and this was his chair I was sitting in.

"Now, play something for me," I said. "Play something you think I'd like to hear."

"What would you like to hear?"

"Can't you tell the kind of music a man likes?"

"I don't know you very well."

"I must make some kind of an impression on you. You must have some idea." I could hear my voice getting thick. I could hear all the heat I was feeling come out in my voice. She must have known, she must have been able to hear it. "Come on, take a chance. Play something that you think is my kind of music."

She turned back to the piano and studied the empty music rack, thinking. I waited. I remembered saying to myself that if she started playing Ragtime Cowboy Joe I'd swat her a good hard one, right across the fanny.

She played another light fingered job that wasn't my type at all. Either she was playing it coy, stalling me around, or she had no idea that there was a man sitting at the other end of the room. It was hard to tell. I was so sure of her and I didn't have any evidence. When she had finished I said, "That was very pretty but it looks like you're going to have to get to know me better."

She got up from the piano. "I'm awfully tired, Mr. Maguire. I think you'd better go."

"Sure?"

"Yes. I'm sorry. I know you're staying to try to cheer me up. I'll be all right. Don't worry about that. You've been terribly helpful. I guess I really don't know what I would have done without your help."

That was me. Good old Johnny. The family friend, always there in times of stress.

She got my coat from the front closet. I saw the closed door of the safe. "You sure you want to leave the money there? You could get a safe deposit box, you know."

"Yes. I'm very sure."

She started to hand me my coat. It was as close as I had ever been to her, face to face. Maybe she was plain looking, but her mousey-colored hair had a lustre. And her eyes were deep. Gray as the lake had looked. Her mouth, even without make-up, was full and red. Waiting.

I grabbed her, held her to me, tight, hard, letting my body feel her body. She dropped the coat and tried to back away from me. The hall was narrow and she backed into the wall. I pressed against her hard. I wanted her to feel the pulse of my body, the tautness of my muscles. I kissed her. Her lips stayed closed to mine. She wasn't fighting. She was passive, not responding.

Then suddenly she opened up and my lips and my mouth felt the fire that was inside her leap out.

Only for a moment. Then she broke free from me, stood away and looked at me.

It had only been for a moment. But I had my evidence. I had all I needed to know.

I picked my coat up off the floor. "You want me to go?"

She didn't say anything.

"You know how it is with us," I said. "You know what's going on?"

She still didn't answer.

"We can't stop it. Either of us. It's just beginning." I looked at her and I suppose I loved her at that moment as much as a guy like me can ever love anyone. Then I walked out of the door and rang for the elevator.

# CHAPTER TWO

was feeling the cold that was in the room now. Except for the bath towel, I was naked and my whole body was covered with goose pimples. I needed a drink. I took a new bottle of bourbon from the cabinet, tore the seal off quickly, pulled out the cork and took a long swallow before I thought of offering any to either of the other men. They both shook their heads when I held out the bottle.

Stanleigh said, "You must have had it bad."

"It wasn't anything like that. I told you, it was all business."

It was a hard picture to shake out of my mind, the picture of her down in the lake somewhere, all that gorgeous stuff floating with the fish. Then I remembered the money. I wondered if the police knew it. If not, it would still be there, nice and crisp, right next to the set of golf clubs. If it was there, only two people would know it. Shirley and me. I had to find out if it was still there.

"You sure it was her?" I said. "You sure she couldn't have just disappeared somewhere?"

"No hope, Maguire. The elevator boy who took her down positively identified her clothes."

"Did she leave a note or anything?"

"No. Not a thing. Just took off her clothes and walked into the water. Brave girl. It must have been cold as the devil."

"You sure it was suicide?"

"Any reason to think it wasn't?"

"No, not especially. I was just wondering."

Stanleigh relaxed a little and settled back on the sofa as though he were planning to stay a while. "It seems she had plenty of motivation for suicide. We questioned her maid and she said that Mrs. Wolffner has done nothing but cry ever since her husband died and complain that there was nothing to live for. Did she give you any hint of what she was going to do?"

"None," I said. "I had no idea."

"What were you doing up there last night?"

"Business, like I said. There were some papers she had to sign."

He waited before he said anything more, looking at me with a half-smile. I could tell from his expression that he knew about the money. He was waiting for me to break. "Go ahead," he said. "Ask it."

"Ask what?"

"About the money."

"What about it? What money?"

"Aren't you surprised we know about it, bright boy? You didn't realize just how efficient the police department is, did you? That's the trouble with you shysters, you think we never know anything. You think you can withhold information from us, don't you? You're just not bright enough. You don't get up early enough in the morning." He picked up the report from which he had read before. "For the last two weeks under a power of attorney you've been converting stocks and bonds into cash. You cashed three checks from three different insurance policies. Last night the elevator man reported that you went up to her place carrying an envelope that appeared to be from a bank, the heavy manila kind. When you left the building, you didn't have it anymore."

"So what?"

"Relax, Maguire. We don't think you knocked her off for the dough. We know about the dough."

"What about it?"

"It's fish food." He started to laugh. "That's a pretty good one," he said. "They always say you can't take it with you. She did. About two hundred thousand bucks, wasn't it? She took it with her." He laughed louder now and the little man who had been silent for all this time laughed, too.

"How do you know?"

"We found some of it, a couple of hundred dollar bills that had been washed up on the beach. We put two and two together."

"What about her?" I asked. "Have you found her?"

"I'm afraid your lady friend is going to be out with the fish for a while, Maguire. It's freezing fast. The lake is going to be solid by night. Her and that dough is going to be floating under ice."

So, that's that. No girl. No money. Nothing left. Nothing left but the yen I still had for her. What a sap I was. I was thinking how I could have taken her last night. The hell with her tears, the hell with her mourning. I could have taken her and had her and maybe part of the fire inside me would have been put out—cooled down, anyway. She might have fought. O.K., so she might have fought. It would have been good that way. Maybe that's what she wanted. Maybe she wanted to get messed up a little bit. Maybe that's the way it was good for her. What a sap I was. I swore then, never again. Never again was I going to play it smart, take my time, wait for the right moment. Take what you can get when you can get it. Like Tina. That was the kind of girl to have. You whistle and there she is and then you whistle and she goes away. That's the kind of a girl for me.

Stanleigh and his stooge stood up. "Well, that's all for now, Maguire. We'll let you know if your girlfriend turns up. We've got men patrolling the beaches. It won't do any good to go dunking for her, freezing too fast for that. Keep your mouth shut about the dough. If it gets out, half the guys in the city will be out there cutting holes in the ice trying to pull it out."

When they had gone, I went to the window, lifted the Venetian blind and looked out onto the street. The street was deserted, too early yet for people to go to work. I saw Stanleigh and the other man leave the building and get into a squad car which had been waiting.

Something was phony. The whole thing was mixed up and somewhere there was an answer to it. There was an answer to her committing suicide. There was an answer to her wanting all that cash at once, then taking it with her. It didn't make sense no matter how I spun it around in my mind.

There would be an answer to everything but there would never be an answer for me. Call it love, call it plain sex, call it whatever you want. I wanted her more than I had ever wanted anything before. I couldn't have her. I could never have her. And she would be hard to forget, the picture of her would keep popping up in my head. And the idea of her, the wanting of her would still be there and I'd have to carry it around inside. No way to let it out, no way to get rid of it.

I remembered that Tina was in the bedroom. Poor Tina. She took a lot from me and never said a word. Funny, you could make love to Tina, you could go to bed with her and it would be good. She would be the way you would want her to be. But with me the fire wasn't there and no matter how nice she was it wouldn't be nice enough. It's like being thirsty when you have a hangover and you keep drinking water and drinking water but the water never seems to hit the right spot, it never gets to the center of the thirst. You have to wait until the thirst goes away. You get hangovers and you get over them. I wasn't sure that I would ever get over Shirley Wolffner.

I went into the bedroom. Tina still lay asleep. I pulled off the covers so that she was exposed. She opened her eyes and looked at me, not saying anything. I don't know what came over me then. I had a feeling that I had to slug somebody or break something.

I unknotted the bath towel and let it fall back on the floor. She put her arms around me and held me as tight as she could. I might have cried, I don't know.

I sure as hell felt like crying.

# CHAPTER THREE

I lay back on the bed, breathing heavily. I felt better. I knew it would not last long, but for the time I felt better. Tina was laughing.

"Thanks," I said. "I'm glad you find me so entertaining."

"What time is it, Johnny?"

"About seven-thirty. It's early."

"Yes, isn't it ever? I can't remember your being so very, early in the morning."

"You got objections?"

"No, your honor, just questions." She rolled over and laid her head on my chest. Tina is a big girl with long, blonde hair. Good-looking, damn good-looking. There wasn't a guy in the 36 East State Building who wouldn't give up his best client to trade places with me as far as Tina was concerned. She might have played around with a couple of them now and then but it was never anything serious, it was only for kicks and laughs. Or maybe to get my goat once in a while when I wasn't acting right. She ran her hand down my neck and down my arm. Slowly, the way I like it. Very relaxing.

"You know, Johnny," she said, "you really have a very good build for a lawyer."

"It's because I'm not a real lawyer, I'm a night school lawyer. There's a difference. Don't forget it. No one else does."

She caught a hair on my chest in her teeth and pulled hard. "Did that hurt?"

"No."

"What happened, Johnny?"

"What do you mean, what happened?"

"I think I have been what you call jumped. That is the right expression, isn't it?"

"Any objections?"

"No. I have no objections. You know I never have any objections. It's only that it was a little startling. I've never gone in for the early morning stuff, myself. It's a little rough on a girl," she said. "You know what?"

"What?"

"Someday I'm going to get me a man who is the gentle type. A man who will treat me with tenderness, who will touch me delicately. Find me one, will you, Johnny?"

"You wouldn't like it."

"No, I don't suppose I would. But it's nice to think about. I think a girl should have something like that to think about. It's like having a secret dream. That's my secret dream. I dream that someday a man will come and make love to me tenderly." She snuggled closer. "What's your secret dream, Johnny?"

"I want to become a deep sea diver."

"You do? How very quaint. Most little boys want to be firemen or policemen. Why do you want to be a deep sea diver?"

"I'm crazy about tuna fish."

"I bet it's got something to do with your boyhood. Things like that always do."

"Nope," I said, "it has something to do with my manhood. Does the name Wolffner mean anything to you?"

"Certainly, darling. I'm not the best damn public stenographer in the city for no reason. He's a client of yours."

"Past tense, Tina. He was a client of mine. If you're so damn hot with the typewriter you ought to remember that he got himself killed in an automobile accident."

"So he did. How could I forget? It seems to me you wrote endless letters to insurance companies about it. You know I really ought to send you a bill once in a while. I think I'm a very bad business woman letting my pleasure interfere with making money. But what's all this got to do with being a deep sea diver?"

"His wife committed suicide this morning. Walked right out into the lake and never came back. All the time she was holding two hundred thousand bucks in her hand. Make sense?"

"Heavens, no. If I ever had two hundred thousand dollars in my hand I wouldn't go near water. I'd stay right on dry land, something nice and dry like Saks Fifth Avenue."

"You understand why I want to be a deep sea diver?"

"What was the matter with her, do you suppose? Why did she do it?"

"I don't know. I can't figure it out. The only explanation is that she grieved so much for her husband, she didn't figure it was worth while staying around anymore."

"That's awfully touching. Was she an older woman?"

"No," I said. "Young. Very young."

"Wolffner wasn't, was he?"

"No, but she was. In her twenties."

"Don't say it like that, Johnny. You make anything over twenty sound ancient. I'm just past, you know."

"Yes, I know."

"I'll flip you to see who gets up and goes over to the dresser and gets the cigarettes."

I flipped an imaginary coin into the air and caught it on the back of my hand. "Call it."

"Heads," she said.

"You lose. Go get them."

She gave me a sharp jab in the ribs and called me something uncomplimentary. It was a game we always played, flipping to see who would do something. Tina always did what had to be done. I think she liked waiting on me. She lighted the cigarettes and gave mine to me, nice and dry. She was always careful.

"You know something, Johnny?"

"Huh?"

"I couldn't picture myself married to an older man. It makes me kind of sick to even think about it. Not even for money. I just couldn't do it."

"She didn't marry him for money."

"You're kidding. What else would a young girl marry an old codger for?"

"Not this one. This was love. She never spent any of his money. He used to complain that she would never buy anything for herself, that she never wanted anything. Anything but him."

"Well, then it must be psychological. Everything like that usually is. He must have reminded her of her father or something. You don't remind me at all of my father. He isn't nearly as beautiful as you are. Do I remind you of your mother?"

"You remind me of a bag in Bagdad."

"You say the sweetest things to me. Besides, I don't. I remind you of Shirley, whoever Shirley is. In your polluted condition last night you kept slobbering all over me and calling me Shirley, your childhood sweetheart."

I didn't say anything. I held tight. Maybe she wouldn't connect it. Maybe she wouldn't know who Shirley really was. Why do I have to be such a slob when I get drunk?

"I'm sorry my name isn't Shirley," Tina said. "You were so nice to me last night because you thought I was Shirley. I bet you wouldn't tell Shirley she reminded you of some old thing in Bagdad."

I forced some laughter. "Sure, I would. That's who Shirley was, a girl in Bagdad. Her name was Shirley."

"It probably wasn't. She had a name like Fatima or Cleopatra or ...." Suddenly the alarm clock went off.

I could have jumped up and kissed it. "Oh, my goodness. I've got to get to work. You may be low on clients, Counselor, but I have to be at my office on time. I'm going to take a shower." She jumped out of bed and walked toward the bathroom. It was fun watching her.

I heard the shower start and I was left alone to think about Shirley. Again, no matter how I tried to put the pieces together they didn't fit. There was a catch somewhere. And there was a chance.

There was a chance that the whole thing was a bluff, that she wasn't dead. If she was the girl I thought she was, she had a lot to live for and she wanted to live. I knew that I didn't have anything to go on. If she had pulled a bluff, there was a reason for it, she was trying to accomplish something and almost certainly she wouldn't stay around here, taking a risk of being discovered.

It was a long shot and I was going to take it. I had to take it. If she was alive, I would have to find her. I didn't know how, I didn't know where. But somewhere. Somehow.

The sound of the shower stopped. Tina called out. "How about some breakfast, Johnny? Sex makes me famished. Make some eggs or something."

I called back. "I'll flip you to see who makes it."

# CHAPTER FOUR

About ten o'clock that same morning, I walked into Tina's office. She was taking dictation from a short, fat lawyer in a green suit. As soon as he saw me come in, he raised his voice, started using a lot of fancy words and involved phrases, and saying everything with a loused-up Harvard accent. In a way, I was sympathetic. I've been tempted to do the same thing, put on the dog, make myself sound a lot more important than I am, when there was another one of the building lawyers in Tina's office. It was such a foolish, futile thing to do, trying to make ourselves into something important, trying to appear more successful, pretending that using a public stenographer was only a temporary measure while our private secretary was home with a cold.

Let's get it straight. We were punks. Except for a few, the building at 36 East State Street was filled with punks, dime-a-dozen lawyers waiting for something big to happen to them. I was one of them, the man in the green suit was one. All of us, we were all alike. Our letterheads were all there in the cubby holes next to Tina's desk; nice fancy paper, engraved with the words, "counselor-at-law." And all the stationery had the same address and it all had the same telephone number. There was a telephone service down the hall from Tina run by a girl named Mary. She sat there all day long saying, "Mr. Maguire is in conference. May I have him call you?" Then I would have the pink slip with the telephone message and be down in the drug store waiting for a phone booth to become vacant. I would start out my conversation by saying, "I was tied up when you called..."

Almost without exception, we were the night school boys, the boys who came up the hard way to nowhere. The boys from nice, respectable law schools got the jobs with the big firms and we were left to ourselves, to fight it out, to fight for the lucky break, the one big client or one big case to take us out of the small time.

The lawyer in the green suit was winding up his dictation and his voice was very loud now and he paced back and forth. All of this made no impression on Tina. She just listened and took shorthand. I hadn't made much of an impression on her either. She had given me a casual, dead-pan glance when I had come in and then not looked at me again.

I needed a drink. It had turned very cold. I rubbed my hands together trying to warm up but what really would have done the trick was a drink. There was another desk in the office, an extra one in case Tina needed other help. I looked in the bottom drawer of it thinking that maybe she kept a bottle there for emergency, but there was only the usual assortment of female trivia and the beginnings of a pair of socks Tina had started knitting for me a couple of years ago.

The lawyer finished his dictation and walked past me, out of the office. Punk, I was thinking. Just like me, brother, you're a punk. You've got night school written ail over your face.

Tina had propped the shorthand pad next to her typewriter and was feeding the machine a set-up when I sat down next to her desk. The morning newspaper was on her desk turned to the page where there was a picture of Shirley Wolffner, and Shirley's name above it in big type so that you couldn't miss it. Tina must have put two and two together, she must have known who Shirley was by then. Her reception was not cordial. She had started typing without saying anything to me.

"Hello."

"Hello," she said and went right on typing.

"It's getting cold out."

"Is it?"

"They say it's going to be nine below by tonight." I started to move my chair closer to her but she was typing with a vengeance now, the sound of the typewriter like rapid-fire machine gunning. "I thought maybe you'd need some protection from the cold. I came to offer my services."

"Thanks, very much," she said, "I have an electric blanket."

"I remember," I said and then I didn't say any more. You've got to handle Tina gently when she gets mad. I didn't have the mind for it just then but I figured there was no point in leaving her mad. It was going to be a long, hard winter and I didn't have an electric blanket.

She fed the machine a second sheet. "What's on your mind, John?"

"I thought maybe you'd want to have lunch."

"It's a little early, isn't it?" She was typing again.

"I guess it is. We got up so early this morning, it seems like the middle of the day. How about a drink, then? I'm nearly frozen. It'll do you good, too."

"I don't drink during working hours."

She was plenty angry. She knew about Shirley. She knew it was no childhood sweetheart or anything like that.

"You're not mad about anything?" I waited. "I'm sorry about this morning," I said. "And about last night. I'm a terrible slob when I'm loaded, you know that. I'm sorry."

The intensity of her typing tapered off until finally she stopped and swiveled around in her chair. She put her hands on my face. "You're so cold, Johnny." She took my hands then and held them in the heat of her own hands. I let mine be limp in hers. Ordinarily, mind you, I wouldn't stand for that mothering attitude. But it was important for me now not to lose Tina, too. "Where have you been, Johnny?"

"Walking," I said. "I took a long walk. I've got a tough case that I'm trying to work out. I took a long walk to clear my head. It's getting very cold. They say it's going to be nine below by night."

Tina smiled. "And now you say, 'I thought you'd need protection from the cold,' and I said, 'Thanks, very much, but I have an electric blanket.'"

"O.K., so I'm repeating myself."

She let go of my hands and stood up, starting to walk away from me. "Did they find the body yet?"

It was no use. Tina was not the kind you could fool easily. "I don't know," I said. "I haven't seen the late newspaper."

"Darling, your eyes are very blue and they look very innocent and in spite of the fact that you're a beast, I love you very much."

"So?"

"Your shoes," she said. "They're sandy. Evidence, isn't it, counselor? And a funny thing about that sand. I bet a trained technician could tell the exact part of the beach that that sand comes from. By an amazing coincidence, the sand comes from the exact part of the beach where a woman decided to commit suicide last night."

"All of a sudden you're getting very observant."

"I'm always observant, darling. I can tell when you have holes in your socks by the way you walk. I can tell when you've forgotten to send out your laundry because you start to wear shirts that are much too small for you. And I can tell when you're being unfaithful, too."

"Damn it, Tina, I've got every right to sleep with who ..."

She wasn't excited at all. I had blown my top a little but Tina was quiet and not shouting. "I know, darling. You have a right to sleep with whomever you please whenever you please. And I have no strings on you. I know that speech of yours very well by now. It's your speech, though, Johnny. It's your point of view. Mine may be different."

"Now, you listen to me. I can see ..."

"Forget it, Johnny." She walked over to the file cabinet and took a bottle out of the third drawer. "We have been through this so often and it never gets us anywhere. Have a drink and forget it."

It was all right then with Tina. We were back on common ground and after a little more of this we would be back where we had started. The bourbon felt good inside. I held the bottle tightly, even that seemed to give warmth to my hands. "They're not going to find the body," I said.

"Why not?"

"The lake is frozen. There's not a chance of her being washed ashore until it melts again."

"And the money, too?"

I took another drink from the bottle.

"Which is it, Johnny, the lady or the money?"

"I lost a client, can't you understand that? Is there something immoral about losing a client? I handled the thing stupidly. I should have never permitted her to have all that cash. I should have known she was upset and unbalanced. I haven't got enough clients to let them go swimming in the middle of winter and never come back."

"It couldn't be the money, Johnny. In spite of all the talking you do, I don't think money means that much to you. If you wanted money, you could get it. You could be rich right now, if you wanted to. You know that. All you have to do is to hit Harry Foster and you could get all the money you wanted."

"I told you to lay off Foster. He gets charged what everyone else gets charged."

"But, Johnny, do you realize how much trouble he would be in if you started to talk in the right places, do you know how much it's worth to him to have you be the kind of man you are, the kind who doesn't talk? He'd pay you, he'd pay you anything you'd want if you'd ask him."

"Foster gets charged what everyone else gets charged."

"Your sense of honesty is very peculiar. You shut one eye to his evading thousands of dollars in taxes and yet you won't charge him a bigger fee than you'd charge anyone else."

"He tells me what he wants me to do, Tina. He tells me what to write down. I'm not supposed to know more than that."

"But you do, Johnny. That's the point. You do know more than that and Foster knows you do. He doesn't care. He pays off plenty anyway. A little more isn't going to bother him."

My client, Harry Foster, was a subject about which Tina and I always argued. She had gotten him for me originally. Her cousin's sister-in-law was married to Foster and she had pulled strings to get me tied up with him. Foster is what is called an operator, a real, big operator. Some of his operations were on the up-and-up and some of them were way overboard. I handled real estate deals for him, most of which were all right. A few widows and orphans got screwed every once in a while but that's the way life is, I guess. But I had access to a lot of stuff which wasn't on the up-and-up, shady deals and illegal operations and income not declared on taxes.

Foster liked me and was decent to me. As long as I didn't have to be a party to anything crooked it was all right. All I had to do was shut an eye. The boys in the local treasury office paid me a call once in a while trying to see if I cared to pass on any information or steal some records. They knew everything he was doing but they didn't have it in black and white. I had gone to high school with one of the treasury men, Tom White, and Tom used to come and try to pump me and then take me out and buy me a couple of drinks and warn me to keep my mouth shut about Foster, telling me that if I talked my life wouldn't be worth anything. He wasn't telling me anything I didn't know. I knew that I didn't have a chance of staying alive more than three days after I talked. Tom had said that sooner or later someone would rat on Foster, that they would get the evidence on him in time, they always did. He figured it might as well be someone else who would wind up with a stomach full of bullets. He said it would give the old neighborhood a bad name if it turned out to be me.

Foster knew that they were trying to make me talk and he knew that I wasn't talking. He never said anything about it, nor

I to him. He never offered me any extra money. He sent me a box of cigars every Christmas which I never smoked. That's all. Nothing else.

I guess that half of Tina's family had gotten rich being a stooge for Foster. She couldn't understand why I didn't cash in on him, too. I suppose she thought that if I had dough, I'd marry her and buy a cottage somewhere and that would be that. She couldn't see it my way.

"Lay off Foster," I said. "I know what I'm doing."

"All right, Johnny. You're a sap, but all right." Tina sat down and began typing again. I had a couple more swallows from the bottle. After a while, without looking up from the machine, Tina said, "What was she like, Johnny?"

What was she like? How the hell can you tell one woman what another is like? Could I tell her that she had hit me as a drink hits you sometimes, making you feel hot and good inside? Could I tell her what she did to my insides, how every muscle, every nerve in my body wanted her and how just thinking about her I'd get so excited I wouldn't know how to let it out? Can you tell that to one woman about another woman? Can you tell her that you wanted her so bad you couldn't see straight and that you would do anything to have her? Anything. Could you?

"She was a nice kid," I said.

"Pretty?"

"Not particularly. Nice enough looking. I don't know, maybe she was pretty. Good build."

"That I could have guessed."

Good build. Jesus, my teeth itched.

"Now, what?" Tina asked.

"What do you mean, now what?"

"Nothing." She began typing again.

I put my hand over the keyboard. "You must have meant something. Get it off your chest."

"I said to skip it, Johnny. Let me get on with my work."

"This has nothing to do with us, Tina. It doesn't make any difference."

"'Doesn't it?"

"No. Remember that."

"Johnny, get out of here."

I was angry then. I stood up and walked to the door. "Look, Tina, no matter what you think, nothing ever went on between us. Everything I had to do with her was strictly business. Get that straight. I'm not explaining this to you because I have to. I don't owe you anything and you don't owe me anything. But there was nothing there, nothing went on between us. Is that clear?" I waited for her to answer me. "Is it?"

Although her back was to me I could tell that she was crying. "All right," she said.

"I'm going to get my mail and then go up to my office. Do you want to have lunch later?"

"Rather not."

"Sure?"

She nodded.

"O.K., I'll see you."

"Yes, Johnny," she said. "See you."

# CHAPTER FIVE

The elevator boy was giving me a bad time.

"No one can go up in the Wolffner apartment," he was saying. "Absolutely nobody. I got strict instructions from the manager and he says nobody can go up there. Absolutely nobody."

"Now, look here, kid ..."

"I'm sorry, mister. Absolutely nobody."

"Where do you find the manager in this joint?"

"He's not here."

I showed him my card. "I'm a lawyer," I said. "I was Mrs. Wolffner's lawyer. I've got to get up there. I've got business up there."

"I got strict orders. You got to see the manager. He'll be back from lunch in about an hour. I can't let nobody up."

I pulled a couple of bucks out of my pocket. "You got a pass key?"

He looked around the lobby and then motioned me into the elevator.

"If they find you up there," he said, "tell them that you climbed upstairs, will you?"

"Sixteen floors?"

"You look strong enough to make it. Tell them anyway. I don't want to lose my job."

"They won't find me. Don't worry."

We got out on the sixteenth floor. "How do I get in?"

"Push."

I pushed and the lock gave easily. "They got lousy locks in this building," the elevator boy said. "You could walk off with everybody's stuff."

The first thing which I looked for was her. She, had always sat at the chair by the window and I looked there automatically, half expecting to find her. It might have been a dream, this whole thing. It might have been a dream and I would be awake now and she would be sitting in the chair by the window.

The police had done a good job of tearing up the place, looking for a note or something, I guess. I don't know what I had come to look for. I had come because I had to come, driven there by some force over which I had no control.

From the window I could see the frozen lake and the policemen patrolling the shore—cold, complaining policemen, aware of the futility of their job, waiting for some higher-up to remember to relieve them.

The brandy which I had been drinking the night before was as I had left it, the glass I had used still there, the dregs of the wine in a sticky ring at the bottom. I refilled the glass and walked around the room touching the tables, running my hand over the backs of chairs, my thumb across the keyboard of the piano. At the sound of the piano in the dead silence I looked back at the chair where she had been sitting.

I am no piano player, but I can do a sort of one-finger polka by ear. I stood by the piano and poked out my one-finger polka with one hand and drank with the other. The piano bench was the old-fashioned kind with a top that lifts up and a storage compartment for music under the seat. The music was arranged in three neat stacks, all of it the advanced-beginner classical variety, the kind girls play when they take lessons in high school. I picked up one stack and thumbed through it.

The first three folios were dummies. Underneath them I found what she had really played, what she had really liked: blues stuff, professional copies of blues stuff, all marked in pencil with special arrangements, the writing in a man's hand.

So, that was it. The other stuff was a fake. I knew it. It had to be. Each stack was the same, a few sheets of classical pieces hiding the other music beneath it, the disguise obviously to throw old Joe Wolffner off the track.

The music had been arranged for both singing and playing, whoever had made the arrangements for her had added cues about how she should stop playing and let her voice carry a note over a certain part, flat a note and slide it in another part. The music was well worn and she had been working on some kind of a repertoire for a long time.

I had my first clue now, the first sign which clashed with the picture of the faithful wife and the grieving widow. But what to do with it? Where to go from there? If she had wanted a career, why couldn't she have taken the money and gone off somewhere to try it? Why the pretense of suicide?

There were many pieces of the puzzle left to find. And there was her to find. Above all, there was her to find. I knew that once I had found her, I wouldn't care about pieces of puzzles, that all I would be wanting was to have her.

There was no evidence in any of the music of the name of the arranger or the man with whom she had worked. I knew his handwriting, but that was all. I went out into the hall and rang for the elevator. When it came up I asked the boy if this was his regular shift.

"Sure," he said. "I'm going to night school. I'm learning how to be a television engineer."

"Was there any man who came here regularly in the afternoon?" I asked him. "Maybe once or twice a week?"

"Yes. Sure. Her piano teacher. Some pansy with long hair."

"Do you know his name?"

"George, something. She used to open the door for him and say, 'Hello, George.' I don't know what his last name was. He wanted to give it to me once, said he'd give me piano lessons for nothing. I figured he had something else in mind."

"You shouldn't have been so damned righteous." I started back into the apartment.

"Aren't you through in there yet?"

"No."

"The manager will be back soon. What if he finds you up there?"

"Make a lot of noise opening the elevator door. I'll duck out the back way and walk down."

Shirley's bedroom had really been ripped into. All the stuff was pulled out of the drawers and lying all over the room. There were papers from her desk which had been scattered on the floor. I looked through them but there was no indication of anything. I tried to find some old checkbooks or bank statements, figuring that she had to pay the piano teacher sometime and his name would be there, but I couldn't find a thing. Evidently, she had managed to get rid of everything. She had planned whatever she was doing very carefully and very deliberately.

The only thing left to do was to go through the classified directory and call up every piano teacher named George. There were only two Georges and one Georgio Salvatori. I didn't figure that any man named Salvatori would be much help arranging "Basin Street Blues," so I tried the other two. The first one was a man named George Harper who had much too low a voice to be the pansy the elevator boy had described and the other was George Waycroft.

From the sound of the man's voice who answered Waycroft's phone, I knew I was getting warm.

"Mr. Waycroft isn't here," the voice said. "He's out of town and won't be back for two months."

"When did he leave?"

"Who's calling?"

"A friend of his." I said, "a personal friend."

"What's your name, fella?"

"Billy," I said. "I used to know George years ago."

"Billy what?"

"He'll just know me by the name, Billy. Where did he go?"

"He went to Florida this morning. He's got the most wonderful engagement at a night club in Miami."

"What night club, do you know?"

"The Flamingo," he said.

"Did he go alone? Did he take anyone with him?"

"Gee, I don't know. He said he was going alone. That's what he told me. But you know George. What did you want with him, anything special?"

I lowered my voice back to its normal pitch and said, "Nothing that will do you any good, buster," and hung up.

Between me and Miami there was standing only one thing, money: the dough which I would need to get there and the dough which I would need if I found her. I had to get hold of some money. Fast.

I dialed Tom White at the Treasury Department and arranged to meet him in a half hour at a bar on the north side. I went out the back door and climbed down the sixteen flights of stairs and came out the service door which was near the beach.

The policemen were no longer patrolling the shore. I looked out over the endless hunks of ice which the lake was. Baby, I was thinking, if you're out there, what a chump you're making out of me.

# CHAPTER SIX

There was time to hoist a few before Tom White showed up. I was in a booth way back in a corner. After a while Tom walked in. I motioned to him and he came over.

Let me tell you about Tom. In his own way he's as much a punk as I am. We both came out of a pretty rough neighborhood. A lot of the guys we had buddied with hadn't turned out so well. A lot of them were smalltime swindlers and racketeers and a few of them were just old-fashioned hoodlums.

Tom had worked his way through college and went into the opposite end of the racket from the other boys. They broke the law and he caught them. But one look at him and you could tell he'd never get anywhere. As far as I know he had never made any friends in college who had meant anything to him. He worked most of the time and people always knew that he was a guy working his way through. Someone who didn't belong. When he was out of school, there was nothing to do but to go back where he had come from, to his old friends and to the old neighborhood. I guess he got loaded one night and knocked-up a girl with acne and was forced into marrying her. They had three kids already and another one on the way. He liked his kids all right but he never said much about his wife. One look at him and you could tell that he was a man who was caught. He had that caught expression on his face and nothing helps those guys. Once they're caught, they're good and caught. It's too bad about Tom. He had gotten himself back into an environment that he had tried to outgrow, that he had been able to outgrow for a while. Better he should have been a hoodlum like the others, at least he would have had a sense of belonging then. But this way, he didn't belong anywhere.

"What are you drinking, Tom?"

"Beer," he said. "With three kids all I can afford to drink is beer."

"I'm buying," I said. "Have anything you want."

He smiled. "I still want beer. I've gotten used to it."

We didn't say anything while we waited for his beer to come. After he had drunk half a bottle I said, "Tom, I need dough."

"How much?"

"Lots. A couple of grand, maybe."

"It makes me feel good," he said, "to think that of all the people you know with a couple of extra grand in their pocket, you pick on me to borrow it from. I'm very flattered."

"I don't want to borrow it, Tom. I want to earn it."

He began to take interest. "How do you figure you can earn this money?"

"That's what I want you for. Would they pay me two grand if I told what I knew about Foster?"

"What's the matter, Johnny, are you tired of living or something?"

"I'm not kidding. I've got to have two grand and I've got to get it fast."

"What about Foster? Why don't you ask Foster for it? You've been a right guy to him. He owes you at least that for resisting all our pressure to make you talk. Get it from Foster."

"I don't want to get it from Foster. Once I take anything from Foster he's got me. One thing will lead to another and before long you and your pea-shooter will be out after me. You know that. You know once you obligate yourself to a guy like that there's no stopping. You never get out from under. I'd rather tell what I know about him and take my chances."

"Once you tell what you know about him, Johnny, you won't have any chances. You won't have a chance in the world. You can start kissing all your girls goodbye right now."

"Another beer?"

He nodded and I called the waitress and ordered a drink for him and a drink for myself.

"Did you get yourself in a lot of trouble, Johnny? Sure there isn't another way out?"

"It's no trouble. I've got to look for someone. I need the dough to do it."

"You want to tell me about it?"

"It won't do any good."

"A dame?"

I nodded. "I guess I wouldn't be much good at that," he said.

The waitress brought our drinks and we drank silently. Tom was thinking hard. "You know," he said, "even if you wanted to commit suicide and stool on Foster, I couldn't be any good to you. The only thing the Treasury Department can offer you is protection and then I don't think that would do any good. Sooner or later one of Foster's boys would get you. But no dough. We can't give you any dough and I don't know anybody who wants to see Foster in the clink bad enough to lay out two thousand dollars. You're stuck, my boy. It's Foster or nothing."

He made sense. I suppose if I had had time to think it out, I would have come to the same conclusion myself. There was no way out but Foster. I couldn't let myself think or reason. In my head I knew it was nuts to spend two thousand dollars chasing after a dame who ten-to-one was out in the lake, dead. And if she wasn't, then what? Maybe she had the hots for the pansy who played the piano, maybe she wouldn't want the best part of me. I knew all those things. I knew I was being a sap.

But reason has nothing to do with the way you feel. When a kid wants another piece of candy, it doesn't occur to him that one more piece will make him sick. He doesn't care. He wants that piece. And I wanted Shirley Wolffner.

"Sorry, that I can't help you, Johnny. You knew that I wouldn't let you rat on Foster. I like you too much for that. I wish I had the dough myself."

"Thanks, Tom. I wish you did, too. Another beer?"

"No. You'd better go see Foster."

"Yes, I guess I had."

"Good luck."

"Thanks, Tom."

"And do something for me, will you?"

"What?"

"After you find her, when you get back, let me know how it was, will you? I'd like to know how it feels when it costs two thousand dollars. It should be good as hell."

# CHAPTER SEVEN

Foster is a hard man with a dollar. It comes in fast and goes out slow. So right away I was suspicious when he said yes to the two grand without making me sweat a little bit.

I saw him at his home that same afternoon, right after I had left Tom White. Foster tried to live the life of an ordinarily well-to-do business man. He tried too hard not to appear flashy or showy. He had bought himself a house in a good suburban area. It was a big house but not overly pretentious. The house was like the shirts he wore, custom made and good material but the monogram very small and refined.

He dressed the part of the suburban gentleman all the time. It must have been a strain for him. He was the type who should have leaned toward big checked suits and lavender shirts and hand painted ties. Wearing conservative clothes was hard for him. I always suspected him of wearing wild silk underwear and pajamas, but I guess not. There was a chance the servants would see those and he was playing this role of the country gentleman all the way through. All of it came off all right, even the pine paneled library looked as though the hunt club was going to meet there any minute. I had only gotten a glimpse of Foster's "boys" a couple of times. They don't use the same kind of guns that are used in hunting foxes. In the pine paneled library they were just a little out of place.

All of it was pretty good, though. All of it, except Gladys.

Poor Gladys.

Gladys was the girl Foster had married before he hit the big money. She had been a nice girl, full of fun, a little raucous maybe, but a nice girl. Not cut out, certainly, for the suburban matron. No matter how many tweed suits Foster bought for her, she still looked like a chorus girl in them. I don't know why he kept Gladys around; he paid little attention to her. He kept her as a fixture mostly or maybe as some guys keep a racoon coat which they wore in college, for old times' sake.

Gladys was bored. She hated tweed suits. She hated living in the sticks. And she hated Foster not being in love with her any more. She had nothing to do, no interest or talent for running a household; the housekeeper did that. She dealt out poker hands most of the day and played against herself. In the morning and early afternoon she listened to soap operas and in the late afternoon listened to the kids' cowboy serials and Captain Midnight. In the evening she changed into a fancy negligee and listened to crime and mystery stories. It wasn't much of a life for a woman who had a good healthy itch to live but she stayed around thinking that someday Foster would want her again.

Once, when Foster was out of town and I was working on some stuff at his house, she let it be known that she was available if I was in the mood. She was, she said.

"You're hard to resist," I had said, "but your husband isn't a guy I'd like to cross up."

"Harry don't care."

"We'd better let it pass."

She turned on the radio then. "I'm going to tell Harry you did it to me whether you do it or not. You might as well enjoy it as long as I'm going to tell him anyway."

I never doubted that she would tell him something, so I figured what the hell.

I saw Foster a couple of weeks later and I was feeling a little uncomfortable. "I hear you and Gladys have been hitting it off pretty good, Maguire. A fellow like you can do Gladys a lot of good, put some class into her. Good idea." Then he talked about something else and never mentioned it again.

That was the beginning and the end of my affair with Gladys. The opportunity had never presented itself again and she had never been interested enough to call me at the office or at home. I felt sorry for Gladys. I thought she was really a very nice girl.

I asked Foster for the dough, straight, without any buildup or fancy stories. I just said that I needed the money.

"Sure, Johnny. Always glad to help a pal."

"I need two grand," I said, "and I don't know when I can pay it back. You'll have to consider it an advance on a retainer."

"Don't worry about it, Johnny. Forget it. You sure two grand is going to be enough?"

That's when it really began to smell bad. There was going to be a hitch in it and it was only a question of time before it showed up.

"It's plenty," I said.

He took the cash from his wallet and handed it to me. "Want a receipt, Foster?"

"What would I do with a receipt? This is a deal between two gentlemen, Maguire. You aren't a hood like the other guys I deal with. I don't need no receipts from you."

"O.K." I had the dough now and wanted to beat it for the train.

"Planning on leaving the country? They say it's very nice in Mexico or Italy this time of year."

"No, I'm staying in the country. I'm going South on business, personal business."

"I was going to say that if you were going out of the country there are some friends of mine you could look up. You know, Johnny, it gives me a nice feeling to know that in almost every part of the world there is a guy who owes me a favor. Nice guys, cut off their right arm for me. And always glad to see a friend of mine. They'd roll out the red carpet for you if I asked them."

"I'm going to Florida," I said.

He smiled. "I got friends there too, business associates. You see, Johnny, no matter where you go you're going to run into a friend of Harry Foster's."

"You can relax," I said. "I'm not running away to hide out. I know what you're thinking. I'm not planning on talking to anyone about anything."

"You know, it was only last night that I was talking about you. With Gladys. Gladys is awfully fond of you, Johnny. You ought to pay a little more attention to her. I was saying what a nice guy you are, a real high class guy. I was telling her how the cops keep wanting you to talk a little, dish out some information and how you never say anything, how they can never tempt you to talk. Gladys said that you were smart. I think you're smart, too. Stay that way, Johnny. Stay smart."

"I told you before, Foster, you pay for what you get, for the work I do. You pay the same rates as anyone else. The stuff I do for you is on the level. Whatever else I see, I forget about. It's not healthy to see it. I want it to stay that way. This money won't make any difference."

"Of course it won't, Johnny. This is just a present. From me to you. With love."

"I'll pay it back or I'll work it off."

"If that's the way you want it, O.K. I'm easy to get along with, you know that."

"Thanks, Foster. I'll get back as soon as I can. I'll drop you a note and tell you where to reach me if you need me for anything."

On my way out of the house I ran into Gladys. She had been waiting for me. She was wearing a tweed suit and when she got close I could tell she didn't have a stitch on under it. It clung funny. It must have itched like hell.

"You're going away, huh?"

"Yes, a business trip to Florida."

"I read in the paper where it's very warm down there."

"I haven't thought much about the weather. I suppose it will be."

"You know a lot of people down there?"

"No. A guy I used to know in the Army lives in Palm Beach. If I have time I'll look him up."

"What'll you do in the evenings if you don't know anybody? Won't you be lonesome?"

"Sure. I guess I will. I'll be working hard, though."

"I thought you told Harry it was personal business."

"You didn't miss a thing, did you?"

"I know lots of people in Florida. I used to be in Miami all the time. I used to have a wonderful time down there. Boy, I could really show you around."

"I bet you could."

"Harry wouldn't care if you took me with you. You know Harry."

I shook my head.

"I could use the rest," she said, "and I'm getting pale. I look so much better when I've got a sun tan. Everybody says so. Harry thinks so too."

"No dice, Gladys. I've got to go alone."

"I'm not the jealous type, Johnny. You could go your own way if you wanted to. It's only that Harry wouldn't let me go alone. He wouldn't care if I went with you. He thinks you got class."

"No, Gladys. Not this time."

"You got a cigarette, honey?" I gave her one and lighted the match for her. "You know, Johnny, I could make some trouble for you if I felt like it."

"You could?"

"You think Harry doesn't pay no attention to me. All you guys. You think I'm just a dumb broad who Harry never listens to. I could give Harry some ideas."

"What kind of ideas?"

"Oh, I don't know. I haven't thought of them yet. Lots of things. You're going to Miami, huh? I could tell Harry you're going to see Joe Penicke. He and Joe don't get along so good. He keeps trying to horn in on Harry down in Florida. Harry would get a charge out of that all right. Boy, how he'd feel if he knew you were using his dough to go down to Miami to sell information about him to Joe Penicke."

"You've been listening to the radio too much, Gladys."

She shrugged her shoulders. "It was just an idea. Maybe Harry would fall for it and maybe he wouldn't. But a guy like Harry can't afford to let anything get by him. He don't take chances with no one."

"You're nuts. He'd find out it isn't true. So then what?"

"Sometimes there isn't time to find out what's true and what isn't true. Sometimes you got to act first and find out later. I heard Harry say that many times." She looked at her diamond and emerald watch. "Gee, I got to go or I'll miss a program. What time are you leaving, Johnny?"

"I said, no, Gladys."

"We could have an awful good time together."

"I know we could. But not this trip. Not this time."

"Funny, I just feel like going now. Harry wouldn't care. Honest."

"It doesn't make any difference."

"You might not like it so good in Florida if you go without me."

"I'll take my chances."

She stood on her tiptoes and kissed me lightly on the mouth. "Goodbye, Johnny. Have a simply swell time." Then she went upstairs to listen to the radio.

Poor Gladys, I was thinking. She wanted so desperately to have some excitement in her life that she was trying to create it herself. I wasn't sure that she wouldn't go through with her plan. If she did, there might be trouble. I should have had her on my side just in case anything happened. Like this. If I had had her in love with me, there wouldn't be any problem now. In the meantime I would have to take my chances.

I had only two hours to get back to town, pack my bags, and get on the train.

Poor Gladys, I think she really wanted to go to Florida.

# CHAPTER EIGHT

The next night, I was in Florida, sitting at a table in the crowded night club and my heart was going a mile a minute. There were butterflies in my stomach and there was a tightness in my legs. In a little while I would know. There was a sign outside announcing the opening of a new "chanteuse" but no picture, only the name, Sandra Williams. The same initials, S.W. It didn't have to mean anything. Maybe it was only another coincidence in a long line of them. It didn't have to mean anything, but I wished with all my power that it did.

The night club was a big place with a small dance floor. Across one whole side of the room there were "French doors leading out onto a terrace which overlooked the ocean. The ocean was quiet and there was a big, full moon and a streak of light reflected on the water.

I asked the waiter again what time the floor show would begin and he looked annoyed and told me that it would start in about five minutes. There was nothing to do but to drink and to wait.

The floor show began with a chorus number and I suppose there was a lot of talent but I had no eyes for it. The second number was an acrobatic dancer who stank. Then the m.c. introduced the new singing discovery, Sandra Wilhams, with Georgie Way at the piano.

The pansy piano player came out first, duked up in white tails and white shoes. He played a short introduction, some improvised blues stuff, and I had to hand it to him, he was really good. The lights dimmed and there was only a spot on the mike.

A girl with thick red lips and taffy colored hair started to sing, deep throaty blues, just the way I like it, low down and dirty. She had on a white dress that looked like it had been pasted on her, nothing could fit that close without being pasted on. She was quite a tomato.

And my heart was down there, right around my shoes.

I had been so sure, so very sure.

Yet. Yet, if I closed my eyes and just listened to her voice. I kept thinking that it could be her, that she would sing like that. She could have done something with her looks, painted her mouth up and changed the color of her hair. It was hard to tell, she had on so much paint and the light was so bright on her. I wasn't close enough to see her well.

She finished the song and the spotlight closed and she wasn't there anymore. She had brought down the house. They hooted and hollered and yelled. Then in the darkness, the pansy began the piano again and slowly the spotlight came on and there she was, beginning another song.

They kept her on the floor for twenty minutes. In those twenty minutes I must have said, yes it is, no it isn't, twenty times. I couldn't tell for sure. I wouldn't know until I really stood in front of her, until I would see her without the paint and see her in the light of the night, then I would know. I'd know for sure.

I sat it out for the rest of the floor show, trying to figure out what to do. I thought that I could go backstage and look her up, pretend I didn't know who she was, make a play for her. That might work. Or I could burst in there and say, "I told you. I told you how it was with you and me. I said it was only the beginning." There were lots of ways to go after her but I had to be careful. If it was her, I couldn't muff it this time. I couldn't let her get away again.

While I was sitting there trying to figure out what to do, the headwaiter came over with a note. I was plenty excited. I thought it was from her. The note read like this:

Maguire:

I'm upstairs. Come up. I want to talk to you.

Joe Penicke

That bitch, I thought. That dirty bitch, Gladys.

"Tell Mr. Penicke I haven't got anything to talk to him about."

The headwaiter shrugged his shoulders and left. I put a ten spot on the table and didn't wait for the check. I hightailed it out of there fast as I could and went back to my hotel and called Harry Foster's house.

Gladys answered the phone.

"What the hell are you trying to do to me? What's the matter? Have you gone off your nut?"

"Is something wrong, Johnny?"

"Let me talk to Harry. I've got to tell him what this is all about."

"Is it warm there, Johnny? Gee, I got a new white dress that'd be perfect for Florida this time of the year."

"Let me talk to Harry."

"Harry isn't here, Johnny. He went out for a walk or something. I don't know where he is."

"Put him on the phone, Gladys. Quit stalling. This is no game you're playing."

"I told you, Johnny, he went for a walk."

"He never walked any more than he had to. I know he's there. Put him on."

"I'll tell Harry you called, Johnny, and have a swell time."

She hung up.

I had the operator get the number back. Gladys answered again.

"Tell me what you told Harry, Gladys."

"You got so much money all you got to do is call long distance?"

"What did you tell Harry?"

"I didn't tell Harry anything."

"I don't believe you."

"Cross my heart, Johnny, and hope to die. I didn't tell Harry a thing."

"How does Joe Penicke know I'm here then? How come he wants to see me?"

She giggled. She may have been drinking although I never knew her to drink very much. "A little bird must have told him, I guess. A little bird."

"You bitch!"

"Johnny, I thought you liked me."

"What did you tell Penicke?"

"Wasn't it smart of me, Johnny? I thought over my first idea and I thought it would be much better if Harry's boys down there told him that you were seeing Joe Penicke, that maybe you had a deal on there with him. Harry will believe them a lot faster than he would me. I think it's a wonderful idea."

"Yah, it's great."

"Does the hotel you're staying at have a pool, Johnny?"

It was there, outside my window, with colored lights underneath the water. "Yes, it's got a pool."

"You know what Harry and I did once? Just after we were married? Harry had to be down there on business and we woke up about four o'clock in the morning and Harry says to me, 'Honey, do you feel like a swim?' and we went down, right then and swam in the pool, without any clothes on. Gee, it was wonderful! It was a wonderful night. We got thrown out of the hotel the next day but we didn't care. It was worth it. I love Florida."

"Gladys, listen to me. This is important. Are you listening?"

"Huh?"

"Call off Penicke. Tell him you made a mistake. Tell him I'm three other guys. Tell him anything, only call him off. I'll promise you anything if you do. You can fly down here and meet me. Now. Anything. Only call off Penicke. I've got too much to do to dodge him and to dodge Harry's men. Come down right away. I don't care. Please, Gladys. Please."

"Harry was talking tonight about how maybe we'd go to Jamaica. I've never been to Jamaica. Have you ever been to Jamaica?"

"Please, Gladys. It's important, believe me."

"I'm going to go look at some movies tomorrow about Jamaica to see if Harry and I want to go there. That must be Harry now, I can hear him at the door. Goodnight, Johnny."

This wasn't going to be easy. Gladys' feelings were hurt and I was going to have myself one hell of a time keeping out of trouble. But I had to risk it. I had to find out about Sandra Williams.

# CHAPTER NINE

The piano player gave me the once-over.

"I want to see Sandra Williams."

"She's not here. Anything I can do for you?"

Then I gave him the once-over. "No. Do you know where I can find her?"

"She's not seeing anybody. She's resting between performances."

I pushed my way into the dressing room. It was her dressing room all right but she wasn't there. "All right, buster, I don't have time to play games. Where is she?"

He looked frightened. "You're a big bruiser, aren't you?"

"Tell me where she is and you won't get bruised."

"She went for a walk." This was a hell of a night. Everyone was going for a walk.

It didn't take me long to find her. I went directly to the beach and saw her standing at the shore looking out over the water. The way she was standing, the way the moonlight was on her face, was a giveaway. There was my girl. There were no longer any doubts. There she was for me to have.

She didn't hear my footsteps in the soft sand. The sound of my voice startled her. All I said was, "Hello." She turned and faced me and her eyes were big and frightened. She needed me. She fell into my arms and started to cry. I let her cry. I let her cry it out. Maybe I got choked up a little bit too. It was good to hold her, to feel her tight against me. I didn't know how long she cried. A long time. Holding on to me tight, digging her finger nails into my arm, hard so that it hurt. But it didn't really hurt. That wasn't pain.

It was a long time before I could say anything. "Hey, there. How about it? Are you going to be crying every time you see me?"

She looked up and tried to smile. "How did you find me?"

"I told you that you couldn't shake me. I told you that you were my girl. I don't let my girls get away so easy."

"You shouldn't have. You shouldn't have found me. I didn't want you to."

"I had to. There was nothing I could do about it. Just like the tide comes in," I said. "Because it has to."

She went limp in my arms and fell to the sand. I sat beside her. My nose and mouth were against her hair.

"It doesn't seem possible," I said, "that I could be holding you now. It doesn't seem possible that all that I've been through has really happened. Why did you go away, why did you leave?"

"Don't ask me that. Please, never ask me that."

"I'll tell you what we'll do. We'll start all over again, pretend we never met. I was looking down the beach and I saw a girl standing there, alone, looking out into nowhere. And I took her into my arms and kissed her, like this." I kissed her and she didn't hold back. She didn't hold anything back. It was a kiss now which said everything there was to say, a kiss which said how things were between us. It was a kiss that sixteen-year-olds in love kiss and it was a kiss of passion and animal wanting. It was all those things in one kiss. It was electricity zig-zagging back and forth between her body and my body, our mouths the point of contact.

When the kiss was over she smiled. I didn't want to say anything else. I wanted to kiss her again but she stopped me with her hand against my lips. "You were telling me a story."

"Was I?"

"About a man who saw a girl standing on a beach and took her in his arms and kissed her."

"Like this," I said and made another lunge for her. She broke away quickly, laughing.

"No, you don't, Maguire. You told that part of the story. What happens after that?"

"Lots of things, Lots and lots of things. They kiss again. And then there's more. Years and years of more."

"This girl. What was her name?"

"You tell me, baby. What is her name? Shirley or Sandra or what?"

"I don't know. You name it. Whatever you want. It's your story. You name the girl."

"I'll tell you what we'll do, we'll name the girl Kitten. Well call her Kitten. Is that all right?"

"Sure, if you want it that way. Let's call her Kitten."

"You know why?" I said. "You know how many lives a cat has? Like you, Kitten."

"Don't say anymore. You said you wouldn't. Please, we're starting over. The other thing didn't happen. Forget it."

"Can you?"

"I've got to go back. It will be time for the second show soon." She stood up but I grabbed her arm and pulled her back, on top of me and I lay back on the sand holding her tight.

"The hell with the show, Kitten. We've got our own show, you and me."

"Let go, Maguire. You're hurting me."

I held fast. "Do you have to call me Maguire? I have a first name, you know."

"I know."

"Say it."

"Let go, first. Really, you're hurting me."

"Say it."

She was getting playful, trying to break my hold, kicking her feet and struggling. "Say it, Kitten."

"All right. I'll say it if you let me go. Promise?"

"Promise."

"John," she said. "There, now let me go."

"Not like that. No, you don't. You've got to say it with feeling. You've got to say it with more than just your lips. Put some soul into it."

"This isn't fair. You promised." She struggled some more. Not very hard, really. Just hard enough to be cute.

"Come on, Kitten, with feeling. Like you sing your songs. With feeling, like you have fire inside."

"John," she said, "There, is that better?"

"No. It still doesn't sound right. Try saying, John, my darling."

"You're a big bully."

"That's fine. Say it that way. Say, you're a big bully, John, my darling."

She looked down at me then, her fingers tracing the outlines of my mouth and skimming across my face and touching my ears. When she spoke her voice was low and husky, she was relaxing, beginning to be the way she really was, the way she was inside. "You're very sweet, John, my darling."

When I was through kissing her, I said, "Still want me to let you go?"

"You'd better. I do have another show to do. George will be having nervous tremors wondering what's happened to me."

"You don't want to sing, do you? The hell with singing. Stay here and sing for me."

"Not, now. I can't, really. I have a job to do. Let me up, please, darling."

I released her and we both stood up and straightened out our clothes. I took her hand and we headed back toward the club, walking slowly, feeling the warmth of the night and the fullness of the moon.

"Were you out there tonight? Did you hear me sing?"

"Yes."

"Was I any good? Tell me truthfully."

"You were wonderful."

"I was scared, Johnny. It was the first time in my life I've ever sung before that many people except in the church choir at. home."

"Your voice, in a church choir?"

"Don't laugh. I did very well. I can sing sweet, too. The man who conducted the choir thought I was very good."

"I bet he did."

"Oh, Johnny, don't be foolish. I've known him since I was born."

"So what? If Wolffner had been around you could have known him since you were born, a lot longer."

"Johnny, you said you wouldn't."

"Sooner or later, Kitten. We've got to have clear air between us sooner or later."

"But not now, not yet. This is an exciting night for me. This is a whole new life. Don't spoil it, please don't spoil it."

"O.K. I'm sorry. I know what it means to you."

"Are you going to be out there for the next show?"

"Sure."

"I'll sing for you, I'll sing right to you."

"O.K."

"You're sulking, Maguire, aren't you?"

"No, why the hell should I be sulking?" I guess I did sound a little surly.

She stopped and with her hand in mine pulled me toward her and kissed me. "Trust me, Johnny. Please." I kissed her back, hard and furious. Then I didn't care about trusting or not trusting or cats or kittens. I only cared about having her.

She was gone. With the silky cunning of a kitten she had slid from my arms and had started running, a little tiny thing running toward the lights and the music of the Flamingo. Baby, I was thinking, you're going to get hell tonight.

I walked back to the club, slowly. Taking my time, trying to catch my breath. At first all I had wanted to do was to find her, then I wouldn't want anything else. I knew now that there would have to be more than that. There were pieces of the puzzle left over in my mind; nice, jagged irregular pieces that would have to be put together before things would be right between us. It would take time, I knew that. I was glad for the two thousand dollars in the safety deposit box in my hotel.

I had to remember about Gladys and the thing which she had done. The smart thing to do would have been to go back to the hotel and try to reach Foster and have him call off his dogs before they really started barking. It was risky to go back to the club and take a chance on getting mixed up with Penicke. But she was going to be in there singing, singing for me, looking for me.

When a guy's got it bad, he has to live dangerously some-times. I had it so bad that I would have walked into machine gun fire as if she were there. That's the way it was. It was all heart and no horse sense.

Every table was jammed-packed for the beginning of the second show. I found a place at the bar and was worried that she wouldn't be able to see me but she spotted me right away. I saw her eyes turn in my direction and her nose wrinkled up. O.K., so this is for me. Sing it.

She was even better in the second show than she had been in the first. She was more relaxed, surer of herself. She let the words and the music come out from way down. It was raw and it was hot. Every son-of-a-bitch in the joint must have felt as I was feel-ing. They couldn't help it. That's the way she was.

When the applause had brought her back for the second time and she was singing again, a man came over and leaned against the bar, standing very close to me. "It's not polite," he said, "to turn down an invitation for a conference. How do you know, maybe it isn't even healthy?"

"Shut up, will you? I'm listening to a girl sing."

"I got business to talk to you, Maguire. We got to do it now."

"Are you Penicke?"

"Yah."

"It's all a mistake. Gladys was talking through her hat. I don't know anything about anything, I'm not saying anything. Nothing. Is that clear?"

"You shouldn't act so cute, Maguire. Come on up. If you know what's good for you, come on up." Then he left and I listened to her finish her song. After that number, they turned the lights on full so that you could see all of her and the applause and the whistles were louder than ever. She threw a kiss in my direction and walked off the floor.

On my way out of the Flamingo, two men joined me, one on each side. I didn't have to ask who they were or what they wanted. Penicke was really interested.

"Look," I said, "you tell Penicke I'll see him tomorrow. I've got a date now. It's a lot more important than what he's got to talk to me about. Tell him I'll see him tomorrow." They wouldn't budge, they stayed on either side of me, hemming me in.

"Now, look here, you know Penicke wouldn't like any funny business in front of his club. Maybe between the two of you, you could beat hell out of me but there's going to be a hell of a racket while you're doing it. Penicke wouldn't like that, it gives the Flamingo a bad name. Now, blow, boys, and tell Penicke that I'll see him tomorrow."

There was a whole gang of people out in front now, waiting for their cars. I knew that if I moved fast I could hake the two men. They wouldn't dare try anything. I started to walk, fast. They didn't follow me. I walked until I got around the corner of the building and then like hell to the back entrance where I knew that she be waiting.

But she wasn't waiting and there was no one in her dressing room. Jesus, I was mad. I don't know what kind of a chump she thought I was. I tried to find out from some of the employees where she was staying but they all had the same answer, they didn't know. She had just arrived that day and they didn't know where she was staying.

Miami Beach has a lot of hotels. They've got more hotels than Clayton, Kansas, has people. Pretty close anyway. There would be no chance of finding her until the next night when she showed up for work.

There she was playing games with me again and I didn't know why. I made up my mind that enough was enough. There wasn't going to be any more of this pretending stuff. She was who she was and I was who I was. That's all there is to it. We were two people and we wanted each other. To hell with this fancy talk, to hell with pretending.

I was boiling mad. I was mad at her and I was mad at Penicke and I was mad at his two friends who had tried to be so forceful with me. I was mad at Gladys and I was mad at Foster. And if the pansy piano player had been within 100 yards he would have had a going over that he wouldn't have liked. For all I knew he and Shirley were living together. Maybe he wasn't such a pansy after all.

There was nothing to do but to go back to the hotel and take a cold shower.

After that I tried to phone Foster again. Gladys' sleepy voice answered and as soon as she heard my voice, she hung up. I picked up a water glass that was on the table next to the bed and threw it across the room and listened to it crash in a thousand pieces. Even that didn't do much good.

# CHAPTER TEN

Sometime in the night, a storm started. I was sleeping lightly, moving around a great deal in the bed. First, I heard the light rainfall which built up in volume until it was heavy and pounding against the windows. Then there were great bursts of thunder and bolts of lightning. I got out of bed, lighted a cigarette and stood by the window watching the storm.

Each great burst of thunder echoed inside me. And each jagged bolt of lightning was what I had felt when I had kissed her. There is time for thinking during a storm and I was thinking that I was getting to be too big a boy to play games of love.

There was a lot to think about and there was nothing to decide, no decisions to be reached. Not until I could have her, not until I could have ripped the clothes off her body and known her in her nakedness, would there be time for decisions.

In my nakedness, I watched the storm and I cheered it on. I wanted the thunder to thunder louder and I wanted the lightning to strike with more vengeance. I wanted there to be nothing but the thunder and the lightning. Nothing. Nothing else. Not her. Not her anywhere.

But she was there. Quite suddenly. A knock on the door, a single, sharp knock on the door.

It might have been a trick, a trick which my ears were playing on me. But it came again, the single, sharp knock. I opened the door and she was standing there, wet, soaked through with the rain. When I held her in my arms she was sobbing and shaking and shivering. Neither of us spoke.

When she looked up at me the tears were in her eyes, rain of another storm. There was no questions this time. I locked the door and then took off her clothes. She stood motionless and silent.

The flashes of lightning lighted up the whiteness of her body, showed off the wonders of it. It was there now, her nakedness was there for me to see and for me to know.

One loud sounding of the thunder was the loudest of all the loud sounds, and when she heard it, she screamed and the sound of the scream was part of the thunder, the life of the thunder. And with the scream still in her mouth she ran to me and her hands were tight against the flesh of my arms and her tongue hard into my mouth. There was the softness and the hardness of her body against my body, stripped now, nothing between us, no bars and no barriers.

Still clinging to each other, we fell to the floor.

Outside the storm continued, long after the storm within us had dissipated and was gone. It ended as it had begun, the thunder and the lightning diminishing and the rain falling more softly. By daybreak it had stopped completely. The sun was beginning to be showing through the grayness of the very early morning.

I watched her as she slept, the sleeping kitten. Then, after a while, I picked her up gently, carried her to the bed and lay down beside her. I seemed wide awake, watching her and watching the sun becoming brighter through the grayness.

Then, I guess, I fell asleep too.

# CHAPTER ELEVEN

The heat of the morning sun came in through the big windows to awaken me. Strong and full, rich with its heat. Good after the winter. My body soaked in the warmth of it, every muscle coming alive and wanting to be stretched and to be active. But I did not move. I was in control now, my body would behave as I wanted it to behave, rid at last of the twitchings and the achings and the hungers which it had had for her. I lay without a thought in my head and aware only of the heat of the sun and the good feeling of being whole and wholly alive.

Then I let loose suddenly. I stretched and I twisted and I turned. I let the life which was inside me be alive, act up and flare out. It was good. It was good to find that the ache of emptiness and the ache of wanting had vanished.

I reached out for her, wanting the warmth of her, too.

She was gone.

As suddenly as she had come, she had gone.

But it was all right. I was beginning to know the way she was, and know that there was no use in trying to figure out her actions on any kind of a rational level. She lived as an animal lives, suddenly and by instinct. There was still the fragrance of her. The whole bed held the odor of her perfume. I took the pillow which had been hers and buried my face in it. A guy does funny things when he is in the heat of love. I was no different.

There were still questions to be answered and there were problems to be solved. Sure. There were walls closing in and there were dangers nearing. But that morning I said, the hell with it.

There was the alive feeling inside me and there was the smell of her hair in the pillow. There was remembering the night before in the storm. Nothing else had any importance.

When I was out of bed, walking to the bathroom, I spotted a pearl earring on the floor. I picked it up and it looked so very small in my hand. I held it tightly. No matter what would happen, this much would be mine. Always. It would not be elusive as she was elusive. It was mine to have and to hold, to hold tightly in my fist.

I whistled through the shower and maybe even let fly some barroom baritone. I dried myself with a good brisk towel in front of the window, soaking up some more of the sunshine. Below me, around the pool, the vacationers had already begun to congregate. The lifeguard was passing out suntan oil and towels. A girl about twelve was doing awkward dives from the low board. Four fat women had begun a card game in front of a cabana. Beyond the pool, there was the beach and the ocean, the ocean quiet now after the tempest it had been through the storm.

Standing there, looking out on the water and into the sun, my mind played a funny trick on me. The sunlight wasn't there and the water was not deep blue-green. There was no rich sand-colored sand.

It was gray. All of it was gray, the sky and the water and the sand. It was her window which I was looking through. She was there, in the chair next to me, looking out into the grayness and crying. Crying for him or crying for herself. Not for me. No tears for me.

It made me realize that although I had found her and that I knew her now, knew her as I had lusted to know her, it was not the end. It was not even the beginning, the beginning of my life with her. There were the loose ends to clear up before we could begin to be having a life together. I had to find out about the girl from Kansas who had married a man old enough to be her father. I had to find out about the girl who had taken two hundred thousand dollars and walked into the lake. But who had not walked into the lake.

There was a character named Joe Penicke who wanted me to talk about a client, who would even use heavy persuasive methods to make me talk about that client. I knew that. I knew the kind of operator Penicke was. It was a problem which would have to be cleared up and cleared up fast before it took on big proportions and got out of hand. This was something I could do now. The problems with the girl would have to wait until I found her again.

I put through another call to Foster. This time the houseman answered the phone and I was able to get right through to him without Gladys interfering.

As soon as he heard my voice, Foster said, "Hell hath no fury like a woman scorned, eh, Johnny?"

"Call her off, Harry. For Christ's sweet sake, call her off before this thing gets me into trouble. You know damn well I didn't come down here to give out anything on you. I don't know what the hell Gladys is trying to do."

Foster laughed. I didn't like the sound of his laughter. "How do I know, Johnny? Funnier things have happened than a guy turning pigeon. It would be a pretty good joke on me at that. Here I give you the dough so that you can go South to sell information about me to a competitor. That's a pretty good laugh. Here I thought I was helping you out of a jam by giving you the money and all the time you're going to use it against me. That's pretty funny. Maybe I shouldn't have worried so about your singing to the Treasury boys. That's peanuts compared to the kind of money Penicke will pay. You're out after the big stuff. I underestimated you, Johnny."

"Come on, Harry. You know that isn't true. None of it. I haven't even tried to talk to Penicke. This was all Gladys' doing. She made the whole thing up. She was mad because I wouldn't take her with me. She begged me to bring her to Florida. Ask your boys, Harry. They must know that I haven't talked to Penicke. He's tried to nab me a couple of times but I'm not having anything to do with him."

"You know, Johnny, I really like you. I've always told everybody that you were a real right guy. You keep your nose clean. I've got other lawyers working for me but I tell everybody that you keep your nose clean. Even with me. I always respected you for that, Johnny. I've always told everybody that. I've thrown a lot of business your way."

"What's the pitch, Harry? What are you building up to? What's the song and dance for?"

"I'm just trying to explain to you how disappointed I will be if what Gladys says turns out to be true."

"You know damn well it isn't true. You've got an organization, Harry. You've got boys down here with eyes in the back of their heads. They ought to know what I really came down here for."

"They tell me that she's quite a looker. The boys say that she's a real number. I'm surprised at you, Johnny. I expected something different from you. I always thought that you would go for the classy kind, the college-girl type. This one sings at Penicke's place, don't she?"

"Look, Harry, this phone call is going to cost me the two thousand bucks. Call your boys and tell them to lay off me, tell them it was all a big mistake. Tell them that I'm not talking to Penicke about anything. And make Gladys call. Make Gladys call Penicke and tell him that it was a gag, will you? This is serious. Tell Gladys to tell Penicke to lay off."

"I'm not much of a gambler," Foster said, his voice was slow and quiet as it always is. "I may have some gambling interests here and there, but personally I'm not much of a gambler. Now, the way I've got this figured out is that if I leave you alone down there, there's just a chance that you could be persuaded to talk to Penicke."

"I don't persuade so easy. You ought to know that."

"But there's a dame in the picture, Johnny. A real, live dame who likes a good time and pretty things. All dames do. Money, Johnny. When you need it for a dame, money can be one hell of a persuader."

"Not this time, not this dame."

"If it's not money, maybe Penicke will find another way. He's a bad boy, Johnny. Joe can play real dirty when he wants to. And I imagine that there are a lot of things you could tell him about me and the way we operate and where we operate. I don't know how much you know, Johnny. If you're as smart as I think you are, you know plenty. I never paid much attention to what you saw or what you knew. I always figured you for a right guy. I still think that you are. But like I said, I'm not much of a gambler. I've got to disregard my personal feelings. I can't take a chance on Penicke getting any dope that's going to let him cut in on me any more than he has already. It's a bad gamble, Johnny. I've told my boys down there to keep you away from Penicke. I told them that I didn't care how they did it."

"What does that mean, you don't care how they do it?"

"This is important, Johnny. This is a lot more serious than you think it is. Penicke wants me out of that part of the country in the worst way. He'll do whatever he can to get me out. If he thinks you know anything that's going to help him, he'll get it out of you. That is, if I let him get to you."

"Come on Harry. You're a big shot, too. You know that I don't figure in a deal like this. I'm a punk lawyer. Remember, Harry?"

"Tell you what, Johnny, I've got an idea. There are two men outside your hotel room right now, boys that work for me. They're there to see that you don't get out. Give me time to get word to them. You pack your suitcase and in one hour from now you walk out of your room. The boys will personally escort you out of the hotel and take you to the airport and stay with you until you get on a plane and come back here. Then we can talk about this thing. You see, even back here, I'll worry a little. If Penicke thinks you're anxious to talk, he'll find you, no matter where you go. But if you're back here where I can watch you, I won't worry so much, I'll be able to give you pretty good protection."

"You know what that will make me, don't you? I'll be one of your boys then. I'll be scared stiff to leave your side because maybe Penicke is coming after me. Is that what you want?"

"I didn't start this thing, Johnny. I'm only trying to get you out of it."

"Well, I can't come back. I haven't finished what I came down here for. I can't leave now."

"Not even if your life depends on it?"

I waited and I thought about that for a second. "No," I said. "Not even if my life depends on it."

"She must be quite a tomato."

"She's one hell of a tomato."

"There's no other way that I can see, Johnny. I wish I could figure something else out for you, but I can't. I can't take any chances. We've got a feud, me and Penicke. I don't like Joe and Joe don't like me. He used to work for me. He's smart as a whip. Too smart, maybe. He caught on too quick. He started in down there when he left me. It was the weakest link in our chain. He knew where to hit at the softest place. He's done very well. Too damn well. I was talking to some of the boys here last night and we decided that it was getting to the point where we would all be a lot better off if Joe weren't in the picture at all. We've been trying to decide how to get rid of him."

"Wait a minute, Harry. Wait a minute. I came down here to see a girl. I want no part of anything else."

"It just occurred to me that maybe you could be some help, Johnny. Help yourself out of a spot and us, too. We'd be very appreciative, me and the boys. It would be worth a lot."

"I'm not getting mixed up in this, Foster. I've steered clear of trouble up to this point and I'm going to stay clear. Get your boys to get rid of him. They must have a lot of experience in eliminating people. Get them to do it."

"We talked about that last night. The only trouble is that the boys would be suspected right away. And they're not too smart, Johnny. You can tell them what to do and how to do it, only sometimes they make slip-ups. If anything would happen to Penicke, people would just naturally think that the boys had a hand in it. And the boys aren't too good under pressure. I don't know what they might say if the cops pushed them around for a few hours. We are always very careful not to let the boys know anything very important. It works out better that way."

"What about me? What makes you think that I wouldn't talk if the cops shoved me around?"

"You're smart, Johnny. I bet you could figure out a way to get rid of Joe and nobody would ever know that you did it. You're smart."

"I'm smart enough to stay out of this, Harry."

"Penicke won't let up on you, Johnny. I guess Gladys really made him think that you know a hell of a lot about the way we do business. Having me slap protection on you right away is going to make him even more convinced that you're the man he's after. He can be pretty dirty if he wants to be. It might even be self-defense, if anything happened to him. That's an idea."

"I'm keeping clean. Get that through your conniving head. I'm not doing anybody's dirty work."

"All right, Johnny. Anything you want."

"I want you to call off your boys and have Gladys call off Penicke."

"You haven't been listening, Johnny. I've been trying to tell you that I can't afford to take the chance of letting Penicke get to you. And if Gladys tried to call him off, he wouldn't believe her. He'd think that I had put her up to it. Joe used to be crazy about Gladys but I don't think he is any more. It wouldn't do any good for her to call him again."

"You think you've got me, don't you, Harry?"

"You might put it that way. Johnny. Sure. That's how it is."

"The hell it is. I'll find a way out."

"It could be that you've bit off more than you can chew this time. You're in a tight spot. You're right in the middle. Think it over, Johnny. Maybe what I said will make some sense to you."

"I'm not buying my way out of this by murdering anyone. That's what you want, isn't it?"

"Did I say anything about murder, Johnny? I did not. I said, get rid of. There's lots of ways of getting rid of people." He laughed again. "Like you got rid of Gladys, here."

"The answer is, no. I'll find a way out. All I've got to do is to call the Treasury Department. They want you bad, Harry. They would like nothing better than for me to tell them a few things about you. They'd get me out of here."

"Maybe, Johnny. But I tell you what you do before you call the Treasury Department. You call someone and take out a hell of a lot of insurance. Leave it to that hot tomato you got down there. She'll be rich in no time at all."

"You don't scare me, Harry."

"Don't I? And what makes you think they can make a rap stick? They've tried before. Income tax evasion is a funny thing, Johnny. You're a lawyer. You ought to know about that. They have to have an awful lot in black and white. It's going to be hard to find."

"I can tell them where to find it."

"It's not hard to move records, Johnny. I think maybe you ought to get another idea. You're smart, Johnny, you'll get it figured out right. Smart and a lot of class. If you get yourself out of this thing down there, you'll have a big future here. Think it over, Johnny. You'll see that my way makes the most sense. Give me a call in a little while. If you're running short on cash, reverse the charges. I can deduct it from my income tax as an operating expense, can't I?"

"Sure."

"It's legitimate, isn't it? The Treasury can't squawk about that, can they?"

"No."

"You think it over, Johnny. In the meantime, I'll … hold the wire a minute."

He held his hand over the mouthpiece. "Hang on a minute, Johnny, Gladys wants to talk to you."

I took the phone away from my ear and held it over the cradle. The receiver was wet with the perspiration of my hand. I heard Gladys's voice saying, "Johnny? How's the weather down there? Is it warm enough to …" Then I didn't hear any more. I let the receiver down.

Outside I could hear kids playing and splashing in the pool and the paging system calling out names of people wanted on the telephone. I heard a woman laughing.

I knew, too, how a guy could get mad enough to kill somebody.

# CHAPTER TWELVE

Cautiously, quietly, I opened the door of the hotel room. Foster had not been bluffing. At the end of the hall, on a bench near the elevator, two men were sitting. They made no move or gave any indication that they were aware of the door being opened or of my looking at them, yet I was sure that they had heard me and that without looking at me, they were seeing me. The animal instinct in men like that is sharp, not buried under layers of education, indoctrination, manners and morals.

There was nothing to do but to retreat to my fifteen dollar a day room and contemplate the world outside and curse myself for ever getting mixed up with Gladys Foster.

Nothing made any sense, no course of action seemed to get me out of trouble. No matter what I could figure out I would wind up behind the eight ball with either Foster or Panicke. For a thing which had started as a joke, this was growing to gigantic proportions. For an hour I walked back and forth in the room, planning ways out and then eliminating each plan as being unsuccessful. Finally, I was perspiring so heavily that I took another shower, a cold one this time, but when I came out nothing had changed except that the heat inside me seemed even more intense under the coldness of my skin. I lay down and tried to rest, to relax and not think about anything. It isn't easy, in a spot like that, not to think about anything.

After a while the telephone rang and I jumped at it. I was pretty sure that it would be Shirley, but it wasn't. It was a man's voice. "We've been waiting for you," he said.

"Who is it?"

"Penicke."

"Look, Penicke, it's no dice. You've got the wrong boy. Gladys was making a joke. She got mad because I was coming down here for another dame. She wanted to come down with me. You know how Gladys gets. She was mad because I gave her the gate. She called you and told you that story about me to get even. I don't know what you're after, but whatever it is, I haven't got it. I've got nothing to say and nothing to sell. Is that clear?"

His voice softened. "There's somebody in the room with you, huh? Some of Foster's boys watching you there?"

I spoke up. "There's nobody in the room with me. I'm talking straight, Penicke. Believe me. Gladys was only being funny. I'm not the man you're after. I don't know anything."

"Don't give me the business, Maguire. I'm no kind of guy you can give the business to. Ask anybody around here. They'll tell you that Joe Penicke isn't no guy to give the business to. We know who you are. We know you got an inside track on a lot of records and dope that we need. Foster wouldn't be giving you all the protection he's giving you if you didn't know nothing. How much did he offer you to change your mind and not do any talking?"

"He didn't offer me anything. He knows that I don't know anything to talk about."

"I'll double it, Maguire. Whatever he offered you, I'll double it."

"You've got this wrong, Penicke. The whole thing, it's a mistake."

"You're a hard man to do business with, Maguire. You're making it hard for me. There's not supposed to be nobody around here who's hard to do business with except me. I might get a little jealous if you keep acting this way. I might even get mad. I might even get mad enough to make you talk and not pay you anything for it. We got ways of making shy fellows like you talk. We don't like to do it, but if we're forced, we're forced."

"You can't scare me, Penicke. What if you did try to get me? Do you think that you could get me out of this hotel room? Foster has two men posted outside the door of my room. I can't get out and I've a funny feeling that neither you nor any of your boys can get in."

"I know all about those two men, Maguire. I know all about them. They can be taken care of. I don't worry about them. I'll make a deal with you. I'll get you out of there without a scratch. Clean. Nobody is going to lay a hand on you. A couple of my boys will come down there and you won't have nothing to do with anything. You can walk out of there like a gentleman."

"Then what?"

"Then you come down here and we'll talk a few things over."

"You'll be disappointed, Penicke. I warn you. You're going to find out that I have nothing to tell you."

"I won't be disappointed. And if I'm disappointed, Maguire, you'll be disappointed."

I had to stall him. I had to give myself time to think. "What's your price?" I asked him.

"We'll talk about that when you get here."

"No, you don't. We set the price now or it won't be any deal."

"How can I set a price when I don't know what you got to say? You just been telling me you don't know nothing. If you don't know nothing then you ain't worth nothing. If you know more, you're worth more. We'll settle the price when you get here."

"I don't know. I don't trust you. I've got to have time to think."

"There ain't much to think about. You ain't got any choice."

"That's what you think. I've got other deals. I've got to have time to think."

"I'll call you back in an hour."

"That's not enough time. I need more time."

"In case you've got any fancy ideas about getting past Foster's men, I got news for you. You won't be able to get past mine. I've got every door in and out of your hotel covered."

"Give me until seven tonight."

"Nothing is going to change by then, Maguire."

"If nothing is going to change then you can wait until seven."

"O.K. I guess I can give you until then. But no later." He hung up.

I waited a minute and then put through a call to Tom White at the Treasury Department in Chicago. I was lucky. I got through right away.

"Tom, this is Maguire. I'm in Miami Beach. Don't ask any questions, just listen. I'm taking an awful chance calling you. This wire may be tapped. Foster is going to move his records, all the real accounts of his business. He's going to hide them out some place else. This is all the stuff you've always wanted to get hold of. I know where they are now, but if he moves them, I don't know where they will be. I'll never be any good to you then. Don't try to take them now. If you grab them now, my life here won't be worth two cents. They're at his place in the country. He's got a great big, fancy bookcase that's a dummy for a safe and files. Maybe he'll try to move the whole thing, I don't know. Maybe they'll move the stuff piece by piece. Get a man to cover his house right away. Don't lose sight of those records, Tom. If you're ever going to nail Foster you're going to need those records. Have you got that?"

"What's the matter, Johnny? What's happened? Are you in trouble?"

"A little jam, nothing serious. I had to get fresh to Foster, I had to threaten him. He doesn't think I'll go through with it, but he's not going to take any chances, that's why I'm almost sure that he's going to get those records the hell out of there."

"What kind of a jam are you in, Johnny? Something with the girl?"

"No, she's out of this. She doesn't know anything about it."

"Nothing I can do? I've got the whole damn FBI to use if you want me to."

"No, Tom, I'll get out of this all right. Only if anything goes wrong, if anything happens to me here, grab those records and slap the book at Foster. Make it stick, too. Do that for me, will you, Tom?"

"Johnny, maybe I'd better get our office down there to keep an eye on you. Maybe they can help you out."

"Promise me that you won't, Tom. It would be like signing my own death warrant. I tell you that I'll get out of this all right."

"O.K. I hope you know what you're doing, Johnny. And, Johnny?"

"What?"

"How was it?"

"How was what?"

"The girl? The two thousand dollar lay?"

I laughed. "O.K."

"Worth it?" he asked.

"Every penny of it."

"Jesus, there must be a lot about living that I don't know about."

"You'll do this other right away, won't you?"

"Sure. Soon as I hang up."

"Thanks, Tom."

"Good luck."

"Thanks. I guess, maybe, I'll need it."

I had until seven o'clock to figure out another stall for Penicke. I didn't know about Foster. He might not bother about me again until the next day. He had me pretty much where he wanted. At least he had me so that I couldn't move very far without being in trouble.

I shaved slowly, going over in my mind the ways which there might be out of the mess I was in. It began to look as though the things Foster had said made the most sense. Maybe if I let Penicke get me out of the hotel, once I got to him I might find a way of getting rid of him, pull it off in a way so that I could plead self-defense. I would have the law or at least the sympathy of the law on my side. The hardest men to nail down are those who operate half inside and half outside the law. Penicke was one of those men. Were I to kill him, it would be a hell of a mess and it would mean that I would have to forget about my career and start over again at something else. But it would be a way out. The only risk that there would be was that one of Penicke's boys would get me before the police did. That wouldn't be so good.

It was something to think about. I had scoffed it off when Foster had suggested it. I could imagine myself doing a lot of things but never murdering a man. Now, I wasn't so sure. My back was against the wall.

It would mean getting a gun. The only hope there was for that was that Shirley would turn up in time. She could get a gun to me.

As I was shaving, I worked it out very neatly in my mind. The whole thing depended upon not running away, maybe even calling the cops myself. I had a chance that way.

I wasn't making plans for myself alone any more. There was the girl. She was the important factor in all my plans. Maybe some guys would have said, this is my own neck that I'm trying to save and the hell with love and the hell with Shirley. But those guys wouldn't be like me, they wouldn't know how it was to possess this girl, to know her as I had known her and to live for the time when you would be with her again. That made the difference. The girl had to figure in my plans. She was a part of me—a vital, active part.

I took another shower after I finished shaving. It was the third one that morning. I must have been the cleanest son of a bitch in Miami. If I was going to be found dead somewhere, I was going to make one hell of an impression on the coroner.

# CHAPTER THIRTEEN

The short, quick ring of the telephone awakened me. The bed was soaked with the sweat of my body. I guess I had been dreaming. I looked at my watch. It was one o'clock in the afternoon. I hadn't been sleeping very long. The telephone rang again. I knew right away that this time it would be her.

"Where are you, Kitten?"

"How did you know who it was? Or do you call all your girls Kitten, Johnny?"

Her voice was good, full of being young and being alive. Happy. I had to play along in that mood too, I didn't want to spoil her happiness no matter what kind of jam I was in.

"Sure," I teased, "I call all my women Kitten. Which Kitten are you? Are you the one I went to bed with at twelve o'clock, two o'clock, or four o'clock?"

"That's me, Johnny. All three." She laughed.

"I've been waiting for you. What the hell do you mean by running out on me?"

"I had to think, Johnny. I was so happy and everything was wonderful and … well, it was too wonderful. I couldn't believe it. I had to get away so that I could think, so that I could realize what was really happening to me. I suppose I sound awfully silly."

"I want you, Kitten. I want you bad."

"Now?" Her voice squeaked a little bit when she said the word. "In broad daylight?"

"Now," I said.

"Johnny, I just woke up and I have a million things to do. I've got to buy some clothes to wear at the Club. I didn't have much time to shop. I have a wonderful idea, you come shopping with me. We'll have a marvelous time."

"I can't. Come up here as soon as you can. It's important."

I guess my voice sounded the way I was feeling inside because she stopped fooling around then and said, "All right, Johnny, I'll be there right away. And, Johnny…"

"Huh?"

"Never mind, I'll tell you later."

"What are you going to tell me?"

"Later. When I see you. I'll tell you then."

"Tell me now. Go ahead. Tell me now."

"I love you," she said. She said it simply, almost whispering the words. I knew that she meant it. Then I said the words, too. They were in my heart, easy to know yet hard for my lips to say. But I said them now and for the first time they were words with meaning. I said the words and she didn't answer. I heard the gentle clicking of the receiver on the hook, the signal that she was coming to me.

I put on a robe and brushed my hair. Then I opened the door of my room again and whistled down the hall to the two men who were still sitting there. They looked up, surprised. "Hey, Rover boys, come over here a minute." They looked at each other and then back at me. Finally, they seemed to agree that it was irregular but all right to come over and talk to me.

"In a few minutes," I said, "there will be a lady coming to see me. I don't want any monkey business, you understand? I don't know what your orders from Foster are, but I don't want the lady detained in any way and I don't want her to be at all suspicious of the fact that you guys are out here trying to keep me in. Have you got that straight?"

They exchanged glances and came to a silent agreement between themselves and then one said to me, "O.K. We got orders you can't leave the room. Nobody said nothing about anybody coming in."

They started to walk away. I called after them, "Hey, wait a minute." They came back. The bigger one had a pack of cigarettes sticking out of his breast pocket. I took the pack. "I'm running low," I said. "Thanks very much."

It took a little less than a half hour for her to get to the hotel. She looked so different from the way she had looked when I had first seen her and yet not different at all. Not different in what she did to me. That same old feeling was there.

"Hi, Kitten."

"Hi, Johnny."

I kissed her for one hell of a long time.

"I feel so wonderful," she said. "I didn't know that being in love could make you feel like this."

"Haven't you ever been in love before?"

"Not with you. It's different with you. I feel young and giddy. Nothing means anything except to be with you."

"Is that why you sneaked out of here this morning? Is that why you disappeared without saying a word?"

"I told you that I had to think. I had to have room to think, Johnny. I couldn't have a clear head with you beside me. Knowing you were next to me, made me want you. You can't think things out when you feel like that. I had to be away from you. I had to be alone to get everything straight in my mind so that I could reason the thing out."

"You're not supposed to reason things out when you're in love. It doesn't do any good. It doesn't make any difference."

"I know that. Ever since I left, I was sorry. I wanted to feel you next to me again. I wanted to hear the funny little sounds you make when you sleep. Did you know that you make funny sounds when you sleep?"

I shook my head and smiled at her. It was unbelievable. She was a kid from the country in love for the first time, not spoiled and not suspicious. Not Wolffner, nor anyone like him, could ever have been a part of her life. She was fresh, and in a way, new-born looking, sprung from nothingness into this girl who was waiting for me to take her in my arms. Which I did.

"Johnny, don't do that now. It disconcerts me."

"That's what I'm here for, baby. I want to disconcert you."

"You mustn't. Not until we've talked. We have a lot to talk about, Johnny. There are some things which you have to know about me."

"I know all that I have to know."

"You don't. You don't know anything."

"I know that you're my girl. I don't have to know any more than that."

"You do. You have to know a lot more than that. I can't let you love me, I can't let myself love you until you know about me. You might not want me if you knew the truth."

"No chance, Kitten. I'll always want you. No matter what."

This time, she took me. There were some tears on her face again. Good tears. Sweet-tasting tears. Tears she was crying because she was happy. "I hope so," she whispered. "I hope so."

"Cut that out. No crying. You can't cry when the sun is bright and it's such a beautiful day and I've got my arms around you."

She broke away, went to the dresser, opened her purse and began to powder her nose and the areas on her cheeks which the tears had stained. "All right," she said, "no more tears."

"Come on back here."

"Where?"

I held out my arms. She walked over and stood between them, standing stiff, not going into them. "Now what?" she said.

"You going to play coy with me?"

Then she was there, in my arms where she belonged. "No, Johnny," she was saying and her wet lips were moving across my chest. "I want to love you. I want to love you."

As the heat of the afternoon sun was different from the fury of the storm in the night, so had the tenor of our love changed. We lay there, side by side on the bed, our hands locked together, looking straight up to the ceiling, searching the blankness there. It had been so different from the night before. More gentle this time. Even her body seemed to be different. Last night she had been lithe and tight, grasping and clawing. Now, she was soft and full, yielding and submissive. There are women like that, infinite variety is what they call it, isn't it?

After a while, I said, "What are you thinking about?"

"You'll laugh at me."

"Maybe. Go ahead and say it anyway. What were you thinking about?"

"I was thinking, what if I would have a baby?"

"That's easy," I said. "It would be a boy and he'd be named John Patrick Aloysius Maguire, Junior, and he damn well wouldn't be a lawyer."

"What would he be, Johnny?"

"I don't know. A fireman, maybe. All kids want to be firemen."

"I wanted to be a nurse. When I was a little girl I used to dream about being a nurse. I would be all dressed in white and there would be men dying and crying out with pain and I would go to them, one by one, and put my hand on their foreheads and stop the pain. I would hold their hands tightly and sit by the bed and wait for them to get better. But they wouldn't get better, Johnny. They wouldn't get better."

"O.K., so all it means is that you would make a lousy nurse." I laughed. "The second one can be a girl and she can be a good nurse. What will we name her?"

"Something soft and sweet. Alice or Mary Ann."

"O.K. I'm easy to please."

"We're being so silly, Johnny. We're talking about such foolish things."

I rolled over and lay on my stomach. I reached over to the night stand and looked at my wrist watch. It was four-thirty. "Would you rather be serious?" I asked.

She shook her head. "No, let's not be serious. Let's not ever be serious. I don't want to cry any more. I want to laugh."

So I tickled her. Gently at first and then really hard. She was a good fighter. She held a grip on my arm and I really had to yank to get it free. She managed to get on top of me and stuffed a pillow in my face. I fought free and started in to tickle her again. But she was too fast for me and she slipped through my grasp, beginning to tickle me. Now, me, I'm really ticklish. I couldn't do a damn thing but laugh and squirm and holler and try to get away from her. Finally, I fell off the bed and landed right next to it on the floor. I lay on my back and folded my hands behind my head and smiled.

"Give up?" she called.

"Hell, no, I'm only resting."

Then she stuck her face over the side of the bed. "Say you give up or I'll get you again."

"You'll be sorry."

"Will I?"

She started over the edge of the bed, first the lovely whiteness of her neck, then her breasts, lopping over the side of the bed, both at once, hanging there. Tempting. My mouth started to touch them but she moved with the speed of a tigress and she fell on top of me, pinning me to the floor.

"None of your tricks, Maguire."

"I thought I told you not to call me that."

"None of your tricks, Maguire, my darling."

"That's better. Now, if you move over a little bit I'll be madly in love with you again."

She said, "I like it where I am."

"You're hurting my stomach."

"It's such a lovely stomach."

"I'd like to keep it that way," I said. "Move, lady."

She rolled over so that she lay half under the bed. "Now, are you madly in love with me again?"

"Sure." I reached over and put my hand on her stomach.

"Don't you dare touch me, Maguire. You'll be sorry." She rolled over and now she was completely under the bed. I edged over to her and we were both under the bed, face to face with the intricate design of the bedsprings.

"I wouldn't like to be a bed-spring," she said, "would you?"

"I wouldn't like you to be a bed-spring either, Kitten. I wouldn't like my girl all twisted out of shape like that."

Slowly, she said, "In a way I'm like that, Johnny. Twisted like that, spiraled around."

"To hell with it. We won't talk about it."

"Sooner or later, we're going to have to talk about it. We can't put off talking about it forever."

"Not now, Kitten. Not today. We'll have lots more time."

"Yesterday, I didn't want to talk about it, either. Yesterday, there were so many more things which seemed important. Yesterday, I wanted to forget everything, I never wanted to talk about it and I never wanted to think about it. But I wasn't in love with you yesterday."

"Sure, you were."

"No, not really. I may have thought it would be nice to go to bed with you, but I wasn't in love with you. It makes a difference, being in love. There are a lot of things that I want to tell you, that I ought to tell you."

"Later. We have a whole lifetime."

"Have we?"

"Sure. You can tell me between children. We'll have thousands of children."

"Where do we go from here, Johnny?"

"I don't know. We can go back on top of the bed if you're tired of lying under it."

"I don't mean that. Be serious for a moment. What's going to happen to us?"

"We'll go home. We'll go back where we came from."

"I couldn't do that. Not when everyone there thinks that I'm dead. I had to die that way, Johnny. In a sense, I really did die. It was important. I can't go back. It would mean going back to too many things."

"All right, we'll go someplace else. Where would you like to go?"

"We could go anywhere. We wouldn't have to worry about money. I still have the money, Johnny. Most of it."

"Keep it. I won't need it."

"What about your career? You can't just throw over your career."

"My career can go to hell. It isn't worth the powder to blow it there anyway. The hell with being a lawyer."

"It's not true. You're a wonderful lawyer. Sam always said that you were a wonderful lawyer."

"Sam Wolffner was a shmoe. He wouldn't have known a good lawyer if he saw one. A nice shmoe, mind you, but he wasn't very bright. Except when he married you. Besides you only think that I'm a wonderful lawyer because you love me. Maybe you're a lousy singer, I don't know. I think you're wonderful because I've got the hots for you. Incidentally, are you any good?"

"Once, back home in Kansas, I thought I was going to be a great opera star."

"I thought you were going to be a nurse."

"This was later. Now, I don't care if I ever sing again."

"What do you care about? Do you care about kissing me?"

She kissed me.

"Wouldn't it be nice," she said, "if we could live our whole lives like this?"

"Under a bed? No, thanks, Kitten. Not me."

"I don't mean under a bed. I mean cut-off from everyone. Like we are in this room. It wouldn't matter about what we were or what we were going to be. We could just be the thing we are to each other, the way we are at this minute. It would never have to change."

"It sounds fine only I don't think my back would hold out."

"Johnny, be serious."

"And there's a question of food which reminds me that I'm getting very hungry. I'll call room service and buy you a steak."

"Oh, let's go out. I know a wonderful place we can go."

"What goes with you? One minute you never want to leave and the next minute you're going to take me out on the town. We're going to eat here in the room."

"All right, Johnny."

I started to get up but she held me back. "Wait a few minutes," she said. "Let's not get up yet for just a few minutes. It's so wonderful here. Please."

As she had been talking, her arm had gone around me, her fingers skimming the surface of my skin.

"It may lead to trouble," I said.

Then she clutched me hard and her voice was thick and hoarse with a flare-up of wanting. "Let it, Johnny. Let it." There was fire in her now, there was fire and the darting flame which her tongue was. There was the sound of last night's storm, unheard by any ears but ours. Great unsounded clashes of thunder and lightning.

And outside the sun was just beginning its retreat, the sand was rosy from the reflection of it, and the trees swayed very gently in the soft wind.

It was like that.

# CHAPTER FOURTEEN

The telephone began to ring. I knew without looking at my watch that it was seven o'clock. We were having dinner. It had been a fine dinner, good food and we didn't talk about anything serious. I didn't even try to tell her about the jam that I was in. The whole day had been kind of a dream, for both of us, and I didn't have the heart to bring her out of the clouds.

But now the telephone was ringing and this was the time for talking, this was the time to tell her about Foster and Penicke. She had to know. It would be hard to do, I knew that. There was a lot to tell and a lot which could be misunderstood, She wasn't in the mood to be hearing about Gladys. She would be imagining that there was more between Gladys and me than there really was. It was going to be damn hard to explain my set-up with Gladys and make it sound as casual as it really was.

"Aren't you going to answer it, Johnny?"

"It will stop," I said. "Whoever is calling will call back later."

"But it might be important."

"Forget it. It will stop."

"I can't stand it, Johnny. You can't just sit there and let your telephone ring."

"Sure, I can. It's easy. All I have to do is to look at you. You see, now I can't hear a thing." I took her hand but she pulled it right away again.

"Johnny, answer it. Please. Answer it!"

"Don't get excited, Kitten. It's only a telephone."

She stood up. "If you don't answer it, then I will."

I got tough. "Don't answer it. If you know what's good for you, don't answer it."

She paid no attention, she grabbed the phone and said, "Hello." She listened for a minute and then held out the phone to me without saying anything. I took it and said immediately, "Call me back in a half hour." There was never any doubt who it was.

Meanwhile she had sat down at the table again and was moving her spoon in a circle on the tablecloth. "I'm sorry," she said. I didn't say anything. "You're mad, aren't you?" She looked at me. "Go ahead, say it. Say that you're mad."

"I'm not mad," I said. "You shouldn't have answered it. Did you think it was another woman? Did you think that's why I didn't want to answer it?"

"I didn't think anything, Johnny. It made me nervous, that's all. I didn't see why you wouldn't answer it." She started to get up.

"No," I said, "stay there. I want to tell you a story."

"All right, Johnny."

I lighted a cigarette, one from the pack which I had taken from Foster's man. When I had taken a couple of drags from it I started talking.

I began at the beginning and I went straight through, without holding anything back except about the first time I got mixed up with Gladys. She took it all in, wide-eyed and silently. She flinched a couple of times when I told her about Gladys wanting to come down here with me but she never said a word. I brought her right up to date on everything, right up to seven o'clock and the phone call from Penicke. "That's it, baby," I said. "That's the story, and that's the spot I'm in."

Something had happened to her during the last part of the story, a strained look had come over her face. Her mouth was drawn and tight and the color was gone from her complexion. "I should have known something was wrong," she said. Her voice was very low, the youngness and the dream-like quality was gone. She kept talking. "I've done this thing to you, Johnny. I should have known that I would. I kept thinking that maybe this time it would be different, maybe this time nothing would happen. All day I have had my fingers crossed, thinking that it was too good to be happening to me, that it couldn't possibly last. Then, this afternoon, I convinced myself that for the first time in my life everything was going to be all right with me, that you would be all right with me."

"What are you talking about? You're not making sense."

"I'm no good, Johnny. Does that make any sense to you? I'm no good. I'm no good for myself and I'm no good for anyone who has anything to do with me. I can't help myself. I don't know what it is, I don't know what happens. Something goes on inside me and I don't know what it is all about. I only know that it means trouble, it means trouble for the people near me." She started to cry, hard. I reached out for her hand but she got up and walked over to the window and stood with her back to me. "You're going to die, Johnny."

"What?"

"You're going to die. They all die, Johnny. You won't be any different. They all die." She said some more but she was crying so hard that I couldn't hear any of the words.

"What are you talking about?"

She couldn't answer me. The crying had grown to sobbing and I was a little frightened. She was losing complete control of herself. I went over, grabbed her and shook her but she kept on sobbing. Finally, I let her have one, right across the face. She didn't seem to feel anything but she stopped sobbing and the crying seemed to turn in, inside her body. "I love you, Johnny. I can't help it, I love you."

"Easy, Kitten. Hold yourself together."

Her voice was scarcely audible now. "It's all right. I'll be all right now. Go away and leave me alone for a minute."

I went back, lighted another cigarette and lay on the bed blowing circles of smoke into the air. After a few minutes she was feeling better. She came over to the bed and took the cigarette from between my lips, inhaled once, deeply, kissed me and put the cigarette back.

"It's time," she said. "It's time to say all the things that we've put off saying. I've been fooling myself all day, Johnny. Last night, too. I kept saying to myself that the past is gone, that it was drowned back there in the lake. This was going to be a new life for me here. Then you came to find me and I was scared at first. But last night when I lay beside you I wasn't afraid any more. You made me feel like I haven't felt since I was a kid. I felt clean, almost like a virgin. I guess this must sound funny." She waited for me to say something but I didn't. I wanted her to get it out. Whatever was coming was something which I would have to hear. This was the sooner or later.

"How many lives does a cat have, Johnny? Nine, isn't it? I thought I could be like that. I thought each time I got myself fouled up and dragged somebody down into a mess with me that I could start over again. I had such wonderful intentions every time. I meant to be happy, to make other people happy. Maybe you can have nine lives but they're always the same life. It's always the same person living them and that person can't change. I don't know what it is, a jinx, maybe. You can laugh it off and say that there aren't any jinxes. I've heard that before, that believing in a jinx is like believing in a witch's curse. You can laugh for a while, sure. But when it keeps happening, Johnny, when everything you touch dies, you'd believe it, then, wouldn't you?"

"Say it, Kitten. Tell me."

"They're not pretty stories. They don't make me sound pretty. I'm not exactly untouched, if you know what I mean."

"Who is? I haven't spent my life locked in the YMCA. Things happen. It's how they come out that's important."

"I was young. Too young to know what everything was about. There was a boy back home. He was in the Army and he came home on leave. I danced with him all one evening and everybody beamed at us, my father most of all. It was the typical small town dance in the middle of the war. He was clean and shiny looking, so handsome in a uniform and I was young and pretty, then. Really, pretty.

"It happens as I suppose all those things happen. Instead of going home we went for a ride and the moon was out and it was warm and there were great stacks of hay to lie on and look at the moon.

"After the first time, I couldn't get enough. I'm built that way, I guess. It was all that was on my mind, all that I wanted. Then I discovered that there were other men who wanted me, men who were older and even more exciting than the soldier.

"The soldier found me with one of them. He went out of his head. I don't know what got into him. He had a gun and fired it wildly not seeming to care where he was shooting. The man I was with was shot through the stomach. I wasn't hit at all. When the soldier saw what he had done, or seemed to realize it for the first time, he turned the gun on himself. It was awful, Johnny. You have no idea how awful it was. I didn't think I could ever look anyone in the face again. I thought my father would die of shame. He was sick, really sick. It was what killed him finally, I think. Ever since that time he was no good for anything. The doctor said it was his heart, but it was shame, Johnny, it was the shame he had because of me. It was eating him alive."

I lighted another cigarette from the one which I had been smoking. She was back at the window looking out over the ocean. There was nothing I could say nor was there any way to help her now. This was something which she had to let out, in her own way and in her own time.

"It wasn't the end, either," she said. "There were investigations and questions and terrible scandal. The man, the one the soldier found me with, was married. He was wounded badly but he could have lived. He could have lived if he wanted to live. But he didn't want to. He wanted me to face the shame. That was two, Johnny. That was two and my father makes three."

"And me? Do I make four?"

"There was Sam. Sam was the fourth. Do you think Sam really lost control of his car and went over that cliff? Not Sam. Sam was a wonderful driver, he was sure of himself. He was sure of himself until he married me.

"I went away from home after that thing with the soldier. I went to a convent, believe it or not. I went to a convent and I worked and I slaved and I hated every minute of it. I reached for any man who would take me out of there. There was one, a delivery man. He was ugly and horrible but I played up to him because he was a way out. I did anything he wanted me to do because I wanted him to take me away.

"I ran away with him but they caught us in Omaha. They sent me back to the convent and they tried to send him to jail. I was still under age. I never knew what happened to him. I guess I really didn't care. I stayed in the convent until my father died. Then Sam came and I saw a chance for a new life. I loved my father, Johnny. I loved him with all my heart and I never had any illusions about myself. I knew that in a way I had killed him. When Sam came to Clayton, I saw a chance to live all over again. I saw a chance to make Sam happy and it would have been like making my father happy. Sam was old. I talked myself into it that way."

"Sam loved you," I said. "He was happy with you."

"You only thought so. Sam was a proud man. He'd never let on that he was unhappy. But Sam was ... well, he could never satisfy me. He was patient with me and gentle and I didn't want that. You know what I mean. And night after night he'd try to prove to me that he could satisfy me and prove to himself, I guess, that he was potent enough to satisfy a young girl. At first I used to pretend. I used to make off that I was feeling great things with him. But not feeling anything, being undone and uncompleted like that turned me inside out, made me hell to live with. It used to drive him crazy the way I carried on about it. I said so many things to him that I shouldn't have said. I worked myself up into such a state that I couldn't have felt any emotion no matter what he had done.

"He didn't have to go on that trip. Sam was the sales manager in the home office. He had salesmen covering that territory. He went away because living with me had made a nothing out of him. His car didn't skid and he didn't fall asleep at the wheel. He drove that car over the cliff as deliberately as the soldier put the gun to his head."

I needed a drink and I needed it bad but there was nothing in the room except some coffee left in the heavy silver pot on the table that the waiter had wheeled in. I poured a cup and it was lukewarm.

"All those days after Sam died," she said, "I cried. The tears were for him, sure. Some of them. But they were for me because I'm the kind of a girl I am, because everything I touch is destroyed or destroys itself. I thought of suicide. I thought of it day after day. Then I thought that I could kill the girl I was, that she could walk out into the lake and that would be the end of her and I could create a new girl, a glamorous girl. A singer with money who wouldn't need anything from anybody. I thought maybe that would help, that that would keep me independent from everybody. I want to be different, Johnny. I don't want to be the way I am. But you see what happens. Now, it's you. And I love you. I love you and I never loved any of the others. I always used the others for something. It had nothing to do with love. But I love you, Johnny, and I don't need you for anything except to have someone to love. And now it's happening to you. It's happening to you the way it happened to them."

"You're wrong, Kitten. I can get out of this. It's not your doing anyway. It's Gladys' fault. She did this. Not you."

"But you did it to look for me, Johnny. That's what's important. If it hadn't been for me, you would never be down here. You'd be home where you belong and you'd be safe."

"But I wouldn't have you. That means something. I wouldn't have you."

"Johnny, don't make it hard. Go home. Call Foster and tell him you'll go home."

"Will you come with me?"

"I can't, Johnny. This will happen again, in another way, some other time. I'll love you at first and then something will happen. Something will happen. I'm like that. I can't help it. It won't be any different than it was with any of the others."

"You're talking crazy."

"No, I'm not. For God's sake let me do something decent. For once in my life let me do something that I can be proud of. Go home, Johnny. Please. Go back and get out of this mess. Forget about me. Get out while you can." She began to whimper. "Please. Please, Johnny."

"I won't go without you."

The phone began ringing then. It was seven-thirty. I reached over to pull the receiver off the cradle but her hand was on top of mine, holding it down.

"Don't answer it yet, Johnny. Wait."

"For what?"

"What are you going to say?"

"I'll tell him if he wants me so bad he can come and get me."

The phone was ringing with long, persistent rings.

"He will," she said. "Penicke won't stop at anything. He'll get you, Johnny. Unless…"

"Unless what?"

"Unless you can get him."

"Look, Kitten, we're going to get out of this and we're going to get out clean. My business is with the law, not breaking it."

"What about the police?"

"So what? They can't protect me for the rest of my life. If Penicke doesn't try to get me, Foster will. Foster will never let me out of this now. Foster wants to use me to get rid of Penicke. And even if I kill Penicke, even if I do it and get away with it, what do you think my life would be like after that? I'd be turning hand-springs every time Foster barked. He'd keep holding it over my head all the time, threatening to tip off the police. I'd be caught, I would be one of Foster's boys. What the hell kind of life do you think that is? What kind of a life would we have?"

"Johnny, do you believe I love you?"

"Sure." I did believe it. I believed it with everything I was worth. A woman can't say those things about herself to a man without loving him. When she comes clean like that, you've got to believe that she is on the level. I couldn't think about the other things she had said, about how it would never work out for us together. There was no time. There was the telephone ringing like crazy.

"Johnny, trust me. Trust me for two hours. Promise."

"What are you going to do?"

"Just trust me. Promise."

"Sure, I trust you, but what..."

She grabbed the phone. "Joe. This is Sandra Williams. Wait there for me. I've got a proposition to make for Johnny."

Penicke was saying something.

"He's not asking for more time, Joe. I'll be over right away. He's afraid to talk over the phone. They might have tapped the wires or something. Wait in your office, Joe. I'll be right there."

When she had hung up I said, "What are you going to do?"

"I don't know. I'll stall him. I'll think of something."

"If you let him lay a greasy hand on you, you'll get a going over that you won't forget. Both of you. Remember that."

"You said you trusted me, Johnny."

I didn't say anything.

"You see how it would be, don't you? You see, knowing what you do about me, that you'd never trust me."

"I didn't mean that."

"You may not mean it, but that's the way it's going to be."

"I only meant with him. I know that you'd be doing it for me."

"Goodbye, Johnny."

"Call me. Call me the minute you know what's going on. See what kind of a deal he wants. See if there is any way I can get out of this. But don't promise anything until you talk to me. I'm coming out of this clean. I'm coming out square with the world."

"Goodbye, Johnny. Kiss me goodbye."

I kissed her as hard as I could, with as much behind it as there can be in a kiss. She ran from the room, leaving me to sit it out and to sweat.

# CHAPTER FIFTEEN

Twenty minutes seemed like twenty hours. It was about twenty minutes from the time she left until the waiter from room service came back to remove the table and the dirty dishes. All kinds of thoughts were going through my head, thoughts about her mostly. Now I knew all that there was to know about her. It didn't make me want her or love her less. The feeling I had was too deep for that, too much a part of me now. Yet I could see how it was possible that she was right, that we two wouldn't be good together.

And then I laughed out loud. I laughed out loud into the emptiness of the room and into the silence of the night. I laughed because maybe it didn't make any difference what I thought about the girl, what plans I would make or what decisions I would reach. The time would be coming when I would have to walk out of the room. Then what? A bullet through my head? A ride into the wilderness, one way?

Strangely enough, all of it went out of my head then. I began remembering a town in Germany we had been in once during the war, a resort town. That night 500 of us descended on that poor little town and what a riot we caused and what fun we had.

I was remembering all this when there was a knock on the door.

"Room Service," a voice called through. "Can I remove the table now?"

"Come in."

The waiter came in. "Enjoy your dinner?"

"Yes," I said. "Fine."

He began straightening up and piling the dishes on top of each other. He had it all together when he saw the cup which I had been drinking out of next to the bed. He got that, folded up the sides of the table and then handed me the check to sign. I signed it and told him to wait a minute. I got a dollar bill from my wallet and handed it to him. He thanked me and started to leave.

"Wait a minute!"

"Yes, sir?"

"How would you like to make a hundred bucks?"

He turned around and looked at me, funny. He was a big guy, young. Looked like he might have been a lifeguard through the day. I suppose he ran into a lot of different situations in a hotel like the one I was in. I couldn't blame him for looking at me like that.

"Relax, buster. All I want you to do is to trade places with me for about an hour. Change clothes and let me wheel that table out of here."

"What for?"

"Never mind, what for. How about it?"

"Gee, I don't know. I might lose my job or something."

"A hundred bucks is a lot of dough."

"Yes, I know. So is thirty-five bucks a week and tips when it comes in regular. I'm supposed to go off duty in about ten minutes. This is my last call."

"A hundred bucks buys a lot of quail."

"I'll tell you what," he said, "you punch my card out for me. Then they won't think there's anything funny."

I started to take off my clothes. "Which way is the freight elevator?"

"That way," he said and pointed in the opposite direction of the passenger elevators where I figured Foster's men were still waiting. That was a break.

"Where do I get off? First floor?"

He nodded.

"Where's the time clock?"

"Right by the back door. You can't miss it. My card is the top one in the third row. The name is Ted Finch."

I knew that I wouldn't be able to get out of any of the regular exits. Penicke may have been bluffing when he said he had them all covered, but I couldn't take a chance. I would have to find another way out.

"Come on, Finch," I said, "start shedding."

He took off his white coat, shirt, tie and pants. They didn't fit so bad.

"How about the money?" he asked.

"When I get back."

"How do I know that you're coming back? I don't even know what you're doing. For all I know you're going to murder someone or something."

I gave him fifty bucks and told him that I'd give him the rest when I got back. And if I didn't get back, there were some clothes in the closet. All he would have to do was alter them and he'd have a new wardrobe.

The most important thing in getting out of the room was timing. I had to wheel out that damn table at just the right speed. Not too fast and not too slow. As I went through the door, I was careful to keep my head turned in the opposite direction from the men. I knew that they were there. I could hear them shifting around on the bench.

It was a long, long hall, a hell of a walk before I would get to the freight elevator. It didn't seem that I would ever get there. Every step I took was with caution. I expected the men to wake up any minute and realize what a fast one was being pulled on them. If they caught on, I would be trapped. There was nowhere to turn to, only the long, dead-end hall. I didn't dare look back to see if they were watching me. I couldn't do anything to arouse suspicion. I wished to hell that the waiter had done a better job of stacking the dishes. They made a terrible racket rattling against each other as I walked.

I went as far as the freight elevator safely. I pushed the down button and then I had to wait. I had to wait an interminable length of time. Now, out of the corner of my eye, I could see them. One seemed to be dozing and the other was watching me. He stood up. My muscles instinctively contracted, ready to run. But he only pulled at the back of his pants, then loosened his belt and sat down again.

The elevator finally came and for a while I was out of danger.

I dumped the cart where I saw a lot of others like it standing and found Ted Finch's card and put it into the timeclock and punched it. I looked through the rear door and there didn't seem to be anyone standing around it but I couldn't take any chances. I was too close now to make a misstep. Keeping on the white coat, I went through the kitchen and through the dining room where there were a lot of people eating. As I passed one table a man said, "Waiter!" but I walked right on pretending that I hadn't heard him. There were doors which led off the dining room and on to the veranda and dance floor. Beyond that there was the pool, the beach and then the ocean. It was darker by the pool. I took off the white coat and stuffed it under a chair and walked out toward the ocean.

The hotel beach was fenced on both sides with high barbed wire, protecting it from the beaches on either side of it. The fence extended some fifty yards into the water. There was no way to get to the hotel next door but to swim out and come around the fence. I took off all my clothes except my shorts and tied them up in a ball and threw them over the fence to the next beach. I stood at the water's edge a moment. To my left, way down where the shoreline bulged out, I could see the lights of the Flamingo. I dove into the cold water, and it was really cold, and swam out beyond the fence and then swam back to the beach on the other side.

My body was cold and white and my breathing was coming hard. I put the dry clothes on over the wetness and walked as fast as I could without attracting attention through the hotel and out to where the cabs were standing. Once inside the cab, I told the driver to head for the Flamingo as fast as he could go. When I could see the big neon sign of the club about a block away. I had the driver stop and I walked the rest of the way. My plan was to get to the side entrance and find a hiding spot until she came out.

Suddenly, there were sirens. Sirens coming from the distance and then whizzing by me, police cars and an ambulance following them. They turned in at the driveway to the Flamingo and I started to run. I didn't know what I was running to. I didn't know anything except somehow she was a part of this, and I was a part of this and she would need me.

A crowd had gathered in front of the club; a big, noisy, well-dressed crowd and they all seemed to be talking at once. I tried to stay on the fringe of them. But I couldn't find out what had happened. No one seemed to know. I edged in closer. As I neared the door, two orderlies were already carrying someone out on a stretcher.

It wasn't Shirley.

I got a flash of greasy black hair on the stretcher. I knew right away that it was Penicke and that could only mean one thing.

They lifted the stretcher into the ambulance gently. After they got him in, one of the orderlies got out and called back to the policeman at the door. "Tell them upstairs, will you? He's dead."

A horrible kind of a sigh came from the crowd. They all made the same sound and they made it at the same time. A couple of policemen began walking through, trying to break up the people.

I slipped past the crowd and headed out toward the beach. If she had gotten away, there's where she would be. The beach was open for large areas at that end of town. I started walking. I walked for almost ten minutes. The moon was bright along the shore and I could see for over a mile ahead of me. Emptiness. Then I heard the sound. It could have been my name or it could have been the sound of the wind coming through the trees. But I heard it again and it was my name. I walked into the darkness from where the sound had come. Before I saw her, I felt her against me, I felt her arms around me and her lips seeking my lips.

There was no thought in my head except escape. Escape. There was no questioning and there was no doubting, there was only the instinctive reaction to danger. "We've got to get away," I said. "We've got to make a run for it."

"No, Johnny. Not us. You. Go away, Johnny. You're free now. Go away."

"Did anyone see you do it?"

"What's the difference? I'm not trying to get away. They'll find out that I did it. I don't want to run away."

I grabbed her shoulders and held her firmly. "Think. Did anyone see you do it?"

"No."

"Are you sure?"

"Yes," she said. "We were alone. No one was in the office with us. No one saw me."

"Now, think carefully, Kitten. This is important."

She interrupted me. "Nothing is important except for you to go away. I did this for you, Johnny, so that you could get away."

"Stop talking," I said. "Don't say anything. Just think. Try to remember now. Did anyone see you come in or go out of Penicke's office?"

"No, I don't think so. I don't think so."

"Tell me what happened. What happened from the time you left my hotel room?"

"Johnny, what's the use of all this? I did it, I'm not going to deny it. What's the use?"

"I told you not to talk about that. Let me handle this. I know what I'm doing. Now, tell me what happened from the time you left me."

"I took a taxi to the club. I went to my dressing room and got the gun."

"What did you have a gun for?"

"It was Sam's. He kept it in the house. It was the only thing I took when I left. I had all that money with me and I thought I ought to have the gun."

"All right, what happened next? What did you do after you got the gun? Did you go right up to Pence's office?"

"Yes."

"No one saw you?"

"I don't think so. I don't think anyone was paying much attention. It was early. There were a few people in the dining room and hardly anyone upstairs in the gambling rooms. I passed several people in the dining room but I'm sure they didn't notice me. I didn't meet anyone going upstairs to the office."

"Where did you carry the gun?"

"In my purse."

"What happened then?"

"I went up to his office. He was in there." She stopped for a moment. "That's all," she said. "That's all. I shot him and that's all. I didn't say hello and he didn't say anything. I walked in and shot him." She broke away from me and walked toward the shore, out of the darkness and into the moonlight. I followed her. "It was so strange," she said. "I shot him and I didn't have any feeling. It was as though I were doing something I had done a thousand times before. I wasn't even nervous, Johnny. Isn't that strange? I didn't even have that fluttery feeling in my stomach that I have before I go on to sing. It was just as though I had a job to do and I went in to do it. That's all."

"How many shots did you fire?"

"I don't know. I don't remember. I just fired. I don't remember how many times I pulled the trigger. He didn't say anything. He grabbed his stomach and fell to the floor."

"What happened after that?"

"I heard footsteps coming down the hall. At first I wasn't going to do anything. I was going to stand there and let them find me with the gun in my hand. But I got frightened. When I heard the people coming, I was frightened. There was another door in the office. It led out into one of the gambling rooms. I had seen him use it when I had an interview with him yesterday. I went through the door and there was no one in the gambling room. They had all rushed out to see what had happened. I followed them and found myself back at the other door to Joe's office. There was a big crowd around the door. I got into the middle of it. Barney, he's Joe's assistant, called the police. I could hear him telephoning. I pushed through the crowd and got as far as the door. Barney saw me and told me to get back. He said that this wasn't anything for a girl to be looking at. Don't you think it's funny? He told me that this was nothing a girl should be looking at and I had done it. A girl had done it. Don't you think that's funny?"

"Did you go away then?"

"Yes. I felt a little sick. I ran out the front door and came out here."

"What did you do with the gun?"

"I don't know. I don't remember exactly. I guess I put it back in my purse. I'm not sure. I might have left it in the office. I told you that I felt sick. I don't remember what I did."

"Where's your purse, now?"

She pointed to where we had been standing. "Back there." I went into the darkness and got down on my hands and knees in the sand and felt around until I found the purse. As soon as I picked it up I knew that the gun was still there. I took the purse back into the light and opened it. The gun was there all right and it was still hot. There was also a wad of dough in there that would have choked a whole stable of horses. I took the gun and handed the purse back to Shirley. Then I started taking off my clothes again.

"What are you going to do, Johnny?"

"I'm going for a swim, baby. Me and your little revolver here are going for a swim. It's going to wind up as far out in the ocean as I can swim. Are you sure nobody knew that you had a gun?"

"No, no one could have known."

"Not even that sweet fellow who plays the piano for you?"

"No, I'm sure of that."

"O. K., Kitten, here goes." I started toward the water.

"Wait, Johnny. Wait!"

"No time. We've got to move fast."

"Johnny, there is no point to this. Please, listen to me. I knew what I was doing. I knew what was going to happen. They're going to know that I did it. What's the use in running away? They're going to find me anyway."

"Not if we play it smart, they aren't going to find you."

"Johnny, please. Please listen to me. I did this so that you would be out of trouble. I did this so that you could live. Can't you see that, can't you understand that?" Then her voice became very soft. "In a way, I did it so that I could live too."

I held her against me, the hot gun still in my hand. "Baby," I said, "if I can't have you, I don't want to live." I kissed her and then beat it for the water and dove into the coldness of it. I heard her voice calling my name but I kept swimming. There would be time for talking later. Right then I had to get rid of the evidence.

I swam as far as I could without knocking myself out completely. I knew it would be twice as far back as it was going out. I'm a pretty decent swimmer and I was sure of myself but the Atlantic is a damn big ocean and it goes down a long, long way. When I got out as far as I could, I let the gun drop. One thing which I was sure of was that if the gun was ever found, there would be no prints on it and if they tried to trace it, they would find it belonged to a dead man and his dead wife. As long as Sandra Williams and Shirley Wolffner were two different women, she would be safe. That's all I cared about.

I took it easy swimming back to shore. Every fifty yards I rested for a while. My legs were getting stiff and I wished to hell that I had been in better condition. I swam and I swam and I swam and that damn shoreline never looked any closer for a long time. When I had been younger and gayer, we had used to go for moonlight dips. This really was a good night for it. The moon was full and the water was pretty calm. The glittering strip of the hotel lights stretching down as far as I could see was a hell of a sight if a guy happens to be interested in scenery.

When I neared the shore, I saw her come out of the darkness to wait for me. I lay half in the water and half out of it for a couple of minutes before I had strength enough to move. She was frightened. I guess I must have looked half dead. I was breathing so hard I couldn't say anything and I didn't have strength enough to lift my head and even smile at her. She tried to pull me all the way out of the water. Poor kid. She was really having a bad scare. Finally I crawled to my knees and managed a smile. I motioned to her to go back into the darkness but she wouldn't do it. She kept talking to me and trying to help me stand up. Between the two of us, I managed to walk over to where we had been before. I brushed the water from my body as well as I could and then put my clothes on. I was shivering bad. I could hear my teeth clattering. I needed a good, stiff shot to get me back in condition.

After a while, I managed to get some words out so that they sounded straight. "I'm all right, Kitten. Don't look so worried. I'm all right and everything is going to be all right."

She put her arms around me and pressed close against me. There was a lot of heat in her body and it helped warm me up. "Johnny, you're such a fool. You'll get sick. Li's not worth it, Johnny."

"I won't get sick, Kitten. This is good for you. It builds you up."

"I shouldn't have run away. I should have let them find me in his office."

"What are you talking about?"

"You. I'm talking about you. I didn't want you to get into this. I thought you were safe in your hotel room. I thought you couldn't get out. I thought that I would do this thing and it would be all over before you even knew about it. I had it planned so carefully. I knew exactly what I was going to do. It would have been too late for you to do anything about it. How did you get out of your room?"

"It's a long story and not very important right now. I told you that you could never get away from me, baby. No matter how hard you tried."

"You've got to let me get away from you. For your own good, Johnny. Don't you see that all of this is for you? You've got to let me go and let me handle this in my own way."

"You're not going anywhere. This is our problem. I must have been nuts to let you see Penicke in the first place. I didn't dream that you'd think of killing him."

"If I hadn't killed him, he would have killed you. I know that."

"I don't kill so easy. Remember that."

"What do you mean, remember that? Do you think I would try to kill you? Do you think that's what I am, a killer?"

"Easy, Kitten, I didn't mean that. I wasn't even thinking that."

"I'm sorry, Johnny." She took my hand and Sat down, pulling me with her. I stretched out on the sand and put my head in her lap. She was stroking my face, tracing the outline of my eyes and mouth. "Listen to me for a minute," she said. "It's my turn to talk now. You said that you wanted to be out of the jam you were in, clean. You said that you didn't want to turn killer and spend the rest of your life in debt to Foster, having to jump every time he snapped his fingers. It was the only way you could have gotten out, wasn't it, to kill Penicke yourself?"

"I don't know. Maybe not. Something might have come up."

"Can you understand how I felt? You remember what I was telling you? I told you about the soldier and the man the soldier

shot. I told you about the other man who got me out of the convent. You knew about Sam. Those men died, Johnny, because
they wanted me. In a way, I suppose they loved me. Maybe, in
their own way, as much as you love me. They died because they
loved me, Johnny. This is my chance to give a life, to prevent
someone from dying because of me. It's a way of ending the jinx.
It's important to me. Don't spoil it by becoming involved."

"I told you before, we're in this together. What's yours is
mine and what's mine is yours. That includes trouble."

"If you went away, there wouldn't be any trouble. If you try to
keep me with you, we'll both get caught. It will make everything
I've done come to nothing. There will have been no point in my
killing Penicke. It's a big thing, Johnny. Killing a man is a big
thing. There has to be a big reason for it. Don't take that reason
away. Leave me, Johnny. Go away. Now."

"You're talking out of your head. I'm not leaving you. Get
that straight. Not for one minute am I leaving you."

Her hands stopped stroking my face. She stood up and my
head fell back into the sand. She stood over me, looking down.
"You think that you're being such a big, strong man, don't you?
You're making the big sacrifice? You're giving everything up for
love? You're going to shield me, you're going to protect me? You
can't leave me alone because it hurts you to see a woman with as
much guts as a man. You can't stand to see a woman being stronger than you. That's it, isn't it? You're not being strong, you're
being selfish."

"Shut up," I said. "I'm getting mad."

"Go on, Johnny, get mad. It's the truth. You're spoiling my
one chance to do something decent in my life. If you let me
go through with this, you think you'll be weak. You won't be,
Johnny. It's what I want. It will put an end to all those other
things. It will be the end of my jinx. If you think it's weakness to
leave me now, be weak then, please. Be weak so I can be strong.
Do you think I don't want you? Do you think it isn't hard to stand

here and talk to you when all the time I want to be in your arms, when I want you to hold me and kiss me so hard that it hurts? Do you think I don't want to feel all those things? Let me be strong, Johnny. Please. Please."

"Look. All this talk about being weak and being strong is a lot of baloney. It doesn't mean anything. There's only one thing that means anything and that's you and me being together. I don't give a God damn about anything else. We're not playing a game. This is our life. Remember that. This is our life and it's no game. I went to a hell of a lot of trouble to find you, I'm not giving up so easy. We can get out of this. If what you told me about the shooting is true, we've got a damn good chance of getting out. They've got no reason to suspect you for anything." I was standing up now, talking big, letting her have it hot and heavy. I was mad and I was determined. All the Irish that there is in me was up and fighting. "We're going back there, you and me. You're going back and do your show like nothing happened. We're going to stay in Miami until this thing cools off. It will cool off. Just watch it. They're going to think it's a killing of one racketeer by another racketeer. The police don't care a hell of a lot about those kinds of killings. Watch what happens. For a couple of days, the story will be on the front pages. Pretty soon they'll start putting it inside. I'll lay dough within a week or so, you can read the newspapers from front to back and there won't be a word about Joe Penicke in it. Then we'll blow town. We'll go away somewhere. We talked about it this afternoon. We were going to do it anyway. We were going someplace new to start all over again. That means something to me. Starting a new life with you means something to me."

"I tried that once, Johnny, remember? I was the girl who walked out into the lake and never came back. I was going to start all over again. The horrible person I was was supposed to have drowned out there. I was going to be someone all new. I was going to be good this time. I was going to be happy. It was going to be the end of trouble, for me and for the people I touched. It doesn't work. Look at me, Johnny. I'm the proof. It doesn't work. It never works."

"This time it's going to work. This time it's going to be different. I'll make it work."

"Johnny, you're such a terrible fool. I love you and you're such a terrible fool. Do you really think it would work out for us? Do you? Do you think you could live with a woman who is capable of murder? I'm seeing things as they are, Johnny, not as I want them to be. I want them to be like you say, starting over and being happy. But I'm seeing the way it's really going to be for us. There would be more trouble. We wouldn't be able to help it. We wouldn't want it to happen. We'd try not to let it happen. But it would. No matter what, it would."

I started to say something but she put her hand over my lips and kept on talking. "Maybe it would be all right at first. It would be exciting. But we'd be hunted, Johnny. Whether they were looking for us or not, we'd be hunted. We'd feel hunted. We'd get tired of different names and lying about the past. We'd know that sooner or later the truth would come out, that they would know who killed Penicke. That would hang over us all the time. You know what you would be to me then? You would be a man I had to commit murder for. I'd hate you for making me that. And I would be someone you were stuck with, someone you had to protect and could never stop protecting. You would think you owed your life to me and you'd hate that. Johnny, I've got the power to see things clearly, to see the truth. It must mean something. This power must have been given to me at this time for some reason. It's going to be the way I say it is. I know it."

She was talking fast and hard. Her hands had a tight grip on my arms and I felt the pressure of her nails digging into me. She was trying desperately to make me leave her but I knew that no matter what she said and no matter what kind of a life there was going to be for us, I couldn't leave her.

"Johnny, please. Listen to what I'm saying. Don't make it hard for me, no harder than it is. Do you think that I really want you to go away? Don't you think that I want you to take me in your arms and hide me, protect me? But I love you. I love you so much that your life means more to me than anything, more than my own life. What happens to me doesn't matter. It's you, Johnny. It's what happens to you that's important. I want you to go away because I love you. Can't you understand that? It's because I love you."

"If you love me, we belong together. That's all I understand."

The grip of her hands relaxed and when she spoke her voice was quiet, but there was an icy quality in it, the quality of thin ice. "I've killed a man," she said. "With my own hands, I've killed a man. That isn't an easy thing to do. You have to love or hate very much to kill. That's how much I love you, Johnny. I love you so much that I killed a man so that you could live. It won't mean anything unless you go away and let me finish this thing in my own way. It's the only way we can go on loving each other. Please believe what I say."

A man has two parts. There is the part of him which is his intellect and his reason. And there is the part of him which is directed from some unknown source, the part of man which is the unbridled animal, the part of man which is loving and hating, wanting and not wanting. I listened to her words, I listened to her words with a part of me which is intellect and reason. They made sense. What she was saying may well have been the way it would be for us. But it didn't make any difference. I had to do what the animal in me was wanting to do. To escape with her and to protect her. To love her. There was no other way.

"I don't care what you know," I said. "You're going to listen to me and do as I say. I'll go back to the Flamingo with you. Go right to your dressing room and get into whatever dress you were planning to wear tonight. Maybe the police have closed the joint. I don't know. If they have, go to your hotel. If they haven't, you go on with your show. Is that clear?"

"What I think and what I feel doesn't make any difference to you, does it?"

I grabbed her and kissed her hard. Then I pushed her away, just as hard. "Does that mean anything? Do you feel anything now?" She didn't say anything. I pulled her to me again and this time I really let her have it, with my mouth and with my body digging into her so that she could feel this throbbing thing inside me. She resisted at first. She didn't want to respond. But there was one truth between us, one truth that would never be untrue. Whatever this animal thing inside me was, there was something inside her that was a mate for it. I felt that nothing could ever change that. It had to be brought alive again. It had to live and burn its own fire and be electric with its own voltage.

I couldn't stop it and she couldn't stop it. In the middle of this second kiss, she gave up resisting. Her fire came out to meet my fire, and the passion inside her was unleashed once more to strike at me through my mouth and ricochet through my body. Then I knew that it was all right. That she would do as I was telling her to do. We would escape.

When we broke the clinch for a breath, she whispered, "I tried, Johnny. God knows that I tried. Remember that, always. Remember that I tried to save you." Then her mouth was against mine again. Brother, that was something I didn't want to be saved from.

I briefed her again on what she was supposed to do. "You're sure it's all clear?"

"Yes, Johnny."

"I'll be around the club for a while, just to see what's happening. If everything is all right, I'll go back to my hotel. If the police ask you any questions, tell them that you ran into Penicke's office after you heard the shots. If they ask you what you did after that, tell them that the sight of blood makes you sick and that you came out on the beach to get some air and that you stayed there until you felt better." She was still holding on to me for all she was worth. "As soon as you're through at the club, go back to your hotel and call me. I'll be in my room."

"Let me come to you, Johnny. Don't make me go back to my hotel. Let me come to you right away."

"Do as I say. Don't come to my room unless you call me first. If someone else besides me answers my phone, hang up. Remember that. If you hear anybody's voice but mine, hang up."

She let go of me. "Why, Johnny? Why should there be anything wrong with you?"

"There won't be. I don't want to take any chances, that's all."

"I know what you're thinking. They're going to think that you did it, aren't they?"

"No. Why should they?"

"Someone is going to tell them about you, that you and Penicke were having trouble. I bet Barney knows about you. What if he tells the police?"

"So what if he does? I've got an alibi. I was in my room and never left it. Foster's men can vouch for that. They didn't see me leave and if I can help it, they aren't going to see me get back in."

"I'm warning you, Johnny, if they suspect you, if you get involved in this in any way, I'll tell the truth. I won't let them hurt you."

"Don't talk nuts. They're not going to suspect anything. I'm just being careful. I want to cover all possibilities. None of Penicke's boys are going to tell the police anything. Guys like that don't believe in the law, they've got a natural allergy to the police. They won't talk. You can pretty well count on that."

"Be careful, Johnny."

"Don't worry about me. You worry about yourself. Keep your head. Don't let anything rattle you. Now, start walking back to the Flamingo. Don't look back at all. Walk slow and easy. Go on. I'll start in a little while."

"Don't come to the Flamingo, Johnny. What if someone should see you there?"

"No one is going to see me. Don't worry about that."

"Kiss me, Johnny."

I kissed her and then I turned her around in the direction of the club and gave her a little push. She started to walk toward the bright lights. I watched her for a long time, the figure of her becoming smaller and smaller, disappearing sometimes in the shadows of the big buildings, then perfectly visible again in the bright light of the night. I watched her until the shadows caught her completely.

For the first time I was aware of the heavy beat of my heart. For the first time I was feeling the fugitive. I didn't like it. I didn't like it at all.

# CHAPTER SIXTEEN

I stayed in the shadows around the Flamingo trying to find out what was going on. As nearly as I could figure out, business was running pretty much as usual. There was a police car in the parking area but that was the only sign of irregularity which I could see. The lights were on upstairs in the gambling rooms. Through the open windows, I could hear the sound of the dice in the chuck-a-luck cages. I wondered how the police could keep one eye closed to the gambling when they were fifteen feet away investigating a murder with the other eye.

I walked around to the front entrance to see what was going on there. Nothing seemed out of the ordinary, except for a photographer snapping flash pictures of the club entrance. A man came out and gave some orders to the doorman. The man must have been the one named Barney. At any rate he was the one who had taken over the running of the place. I could tell by the doorman's quick obedience and very polite tone. I wish I had known about Barney. I wish I had known just how much he knew about me. But I would have to take my chances with him and hope that if he knew anything, he wouldn't talk.

I walked around to the other side of the club, the side where the terrace is. The big doors were open and I could hear the music and see part of the dance floor where the floorshow was going on. I found a good spot in the darkness and lighted a cigarette. I could catch an occasional glimpse of the acrobatic dancer. I waited to see if Shirley would appear. There was some applause for the dancer and then a few minutes of silence. I heard the piano begin the introduction to her song and then the sound of her voice crying through a blues number. The direction of the wind was varying. Sometimes I could hear her as plainly as if she were standing next to me and at other times I couldn't hear her at all. There was no sound but the sound of the wind itself. But what I did hear of her singing was good. She sang with a lot of assurance and I figured everything had gone off without a hitch. I listened all the way through her first number and decided that I had better not run my luck any more. It was a risk being out of the hotel. If anyone found out that I had left my room, it would mean the end of my perfect alibi. Perfect, that is, except for the waiter from room service. He would have to be dealt with in some way. I didn't know how. I knew what people mean when they say one murder leads to another. Murdering the waiter was my only assurance of a perfect alibi but I had had enough of murder that night. I knew that I would have to think of something else. I had to get back into my room exactly the way in which I had left it.

I still thought it was too much of a risk walking in through the hotel lobby so I got out of the cab at the hotel next to mine, went through that hotel to the beach, took off my clothes and threw them over the fence, swam out around the fence and came back on the beach of my own hotel. The waiter's white coat was where I had hidden it under the chair. I put it on, went through the now deserted dining room. I had to find something to carry up to my room. I still needed a drink so I thought that I would knock off two birds with one stone. I found a tray in the kitchen and poked around until I found the room service bar. I ordered a double scotch for room 816. The bartender looked at me and asked me if I was new at the hotel and I told him that I was. I took the tray and the check and went through the cashier who was reading a two-bit novel and didn't even take time to look up at me.

The man who was running the freight elevator was in a talking mood and he took his time getting up to the eighth floor. I heard about union dues and how much better off he would be working for a small salary and tips, and how this weather wasn't all that it was supposed to be, and he thought maybe next year he would take his arthritis and go to California.

Foster's two men were still in the hall. They looked up when they heard the sound of the freight elevator door being opened. I held the tray up so that it screened part of my face and walked to the door of my room, knocked loud and called, "Room service." After a few seconds I heard the door being unlocked and I went in quickly. Before I said anything to the waiter, I swallowed the double scotch. Once it was inside, I was in better shape. "How did it go?"

"Where the hell have you been? I thought you'd never get back. You said it would take only an hour. You've been gone over an hour and a half. I got a date. My girl's waiting for me."

"What happened? Anything?"

"The phone rang a couple of times. I didn't answer it. You didn't say nothing about answering it so I let it ring."

"Anything else?"

"No. How about the other fifty? I got to scram."

I gave him the rest of the money. He put on the white coat and took the tray and empty glass. "How good are you at keeping your mouth closed?" I asked.

"Me? How come?"

"I just asked you a question. How good are you at keeping your mouth shut?"

"It depends," he said.

"One hundred bucks is a lot of dough."

"Not down here, it isn't. People spend money like water down here. It costs a lot to live."

"Well, keep your mouth shut about tonight. Tell your girl that you had to work overtime or something. Just forget this whole thing." I took another fifty bucks from my wallet. "Here, this is so that you won't remember anything."

"Thanks, Mr. Maguire. It's all right. I won't remember anything."

As soon as he was gone, I locked the door and went into the bathroom and took a hot shower. Me and the Atlantic ocean had had a work-out together that night and my body was chilled all the way through. When I came out of the shower, I picked up the phone. The switchboard operator answered. "This is Mr. Maguire," I said. "I've been sleeping for a couple of hours. I thought I heard the phone ring a few times. Are there any messages for me?"

"I'll connect you with the message clerk, Mr. Maguire."

Then I heard another voice answer, "Message clerk."

"This is Mr. Maguire. I've been sleeping and I think the phone rang a couple of times. Are there any messages?"

"What is your room number?"

"816."

I waited a minute and then she said, "I have only one message, Mr. Maguire. You're to call Long Distance operator 43."

"Nothing else?"

"No, sir."

"Thanks."

I signaled the switchboard and was put through to long distance. Operator 43 rang Chicago and in a few seconds I was talking to Harry Foster. "Nice work," he said.

"What are you talking about?"

"News travels fast, Johnny. Too bad about Joe."

"I still don't know what you're talking about. I just woke up. I've been sleeping. I was sleeping when you called. What's this all about?"

"It's all right, Johnny. You did a good job. My boys down there tell me that the police haven't any idea who did it. Some of the boys have been pulled in for questioning already but they don't know anything and if they don't know anything, they can't say anything. I'm proud of you."

"What are you trying to tell me, Foster? Are you trying to tell me that Penicke is dead?"

"Now, Johnny. You don't have to play dumb with me. It was a good job."

"I'm glad it was, Foster. Only I didn't do it. I didn't even know that Penicke was dead until you told me just now. I haven't been out of this room. You ought to know that. You've got your watchdogs out there. They can tell you I haven't been out of this room."

"You wouldn't fool me, Johnny?"

"Wait a minute, Harry. I'll get your boys in here." I laid down the receiver and went out into the hall. "Hey, you guys," I yelled. "Come in here." They looked back and forth from each other to me. "It's all right. Your boss is on the telephone. He wants to talk to you."

As they came into the room, the big one took out his gun and had it ready. "No one is going to hurt you," I said. "Go on. Foster's on the phone. He wants to know if I've been out of my room since you came on duty."

The big man, the one with the gun, motioned to his buddy. "Talk to him, Fred. See if it is Foster."

The man, Fred, picked up the phone and said, "This is Fred. Who is this?"

I could hear only one end of the conversation but the important thing was put across. Fred swore that I hadn't been out of the hotel room since they had come on duty. Foster must have asked some more questions because the only thing Fred said after that was yes or no, until he said, "All right, Mr. Foster. Right away. Just a minute, Mr. Foster." He looked over at me. "He wants to talk to you again."

I waited until the men had left the room, then I picked up the phone. "You see, Harry, you've got me all wrong. Somebody else must have had it in for Penicke."

"Maybe you didn't do it, Johnny, but you saw that it was done. That's what's important. I've got to hand it to you to stay out of trouble. It doesn't make any difference just as long as Penicke is dead. It's going to work out all right Barney down there who used to be Joe's right hand man is coming in with me. I've already talked to him. It's a pretty good deal for him and me both."

"When did it happen, Harry? I talked to Joe at seven-thirty. He was very much alive then."

"It couldn't have been long after that. Maybe fifteen or twenty minutes. I got the flash about ten minutes after it happened. I've been damn busy tonight. I must have talked to Miami five or six times in the last hour. I've got to hand it to you, Johnny. You did this thing real neat. I'm not even going to ask you how you arranged it."

"Look, Harry, you can think whatever you want to. Only I didn't have anything to do with it. The only thing I want you to do is leave me alone from now on. Do you understand?"

"Now, Johnny, that's no way to talk. I've got big things lined up for you when you get back. Big things."

"You can take all those big things and shove them, Foster. I don't want the best part of them."

"I'm sending you some more dough, Johnny. Another two grand. Take a long rest. Enjoy yourself. You and your girlfriend. Then when you get home, you and I can..."

He stopped talking suddenly. He didn't hang up so I could hear parts of what was going on. There was a woman's voice in the background talking loud. I heard Foster say, "You dumb broad, put down that gun." It was Gladys. I heard her screaming at him. I couldn't make out exactly what she was saying. It was something about Penicke. Then he must have dropped the phone. I could still hear Gladys's voice screaming and yelling. Then I heard somebody get a hell of a sock across the face. After a couple of minutes, Foster came back to the phone. "That was your girlfriend, Johnny." His voice was shaking. "She's heart-broken because she thinks I had Penicke knocked off. She's such a dumb broad, that one. I don't know why I don't dump her somewhere. Did you think she wanted to go to Florida because of you, Johnny? Hell, no. She was so nuts for Joe, she didn't know what she was doing. It's one of the reasons me and Joe busted up. Can you imagine any broad being so damn dumb? Once Joe got to Florida he got himself a new piece and didn't want nothing to do with Gladys any more. He told her so. And still she was nuts for him. She still thinks he's the greatest guy that ever walked. And she pulls a gun on me because she thinks I had him knocked off. You don't know how good I've been to her, Maguire. I pulled her out of the gutter and tried to make a lady out of her. She can have anything she wants from me. She knows that. So she pulls a gun on me because her boyfriend got killed. If I had any brains, I'd stop feeling sorry for her. I'd turn her out into the street where she belongs."

There was a lot I could have told Foster about Gladys. I still think she was nuts for him, or would have been if he ever paid any attention to her. Gladys didn't want to be a lady. She was a broad and she wanted to be a broad. Maybe that's why she responded to Penicke. He probably treated her like a broad and she loved it. But deep down, Gladys must have still had some feeling for Foster. She hadn't fired the gun. That meant something. She was probably only trying to give Foster a good scare. But hell, that was their problem. I had enough of my own.

"I got to go, Johnny. Gladys is bleeding pretty bad. I better get her fixed up. Thanks a million for what you did."

"I didn't do it, Harry. Get that through your head. I didn't do it."

"I'll see you, Johnny."

As soon as I hung up the phone, it rang again. It was Shirley.

"Where are you?"

"At the club, Johnny. Everything is all right."

"The police still there?"

"Yes."

"Did they talk to you?"

"Yes."

"All right?"

"Yes." She laughed. "One of them asked me to go out with him later."

"I think it's going to be all right, Kitten. Go through everything just like I said. What time does the last show go on?"

"Midnight."

"Go right to your hotel after the show and call me from there. I think everything is going to be all right."

"I love you, Johnny."

"Me, too, Kitten."

"Later, Johnny? We'll be together later, won't we? Promise me?"

I knew that no matter what had happened it was worth it. She was for me like no one else in the world could ever be. I wondered if I would ever be able to tell Tom White about it. He wanted to know what a two grand lay was like. I was wondering what he would think if he knew that there was more than two grand in the deal. There was the two grand and there was two hundred grand and there was murder. I was wondering what he would say.

# CHAPTER SEVENTEEN

I tossed around the bed for a half hour, but I couldn't sleep. I was very tired but I couldn't sleep. I called room service and ordered another drink. I asked them to send up the latest editions of the newspapers. The story was headlined in all the papers but so far the account of it was brief and nothing was said about anyone being a suspect. One of the headlines read, "Gangland Killing Baffles Police." There was no radio in the room so that I had no way of keeping posted on developments. I would have to wait it out. I took the drink, turned the light off again and made another try at sleeping. It was still no good. I twisted and turned, I thought about a lot of things. I thought about law and what it says about murder and people who are accessories to murder. That didn't sit too good in my stomach. But I was in this now and there was no way of backing out.

I lay there for another hour. The phone rang and I turned on the light. It was long distance again. This time it was Tom White calling from his office.

"What the hell is going on down there, Johnny?"

"Why? What's the matter?"

"I don't know. Everything is going crazy here. All hell is breaking loose. Any minute, the Foster case is going to bust wide open. The police have got Foster's wife in custody and she's singing like a canary. She turned up at headquarters badly beat-up and said that she had some information on a killing in Miami. She said that her husband engineered the murder of a man down there. Boy, she's really mad at her husband. She offered to turn in all kinds of evidence, the stuff we've been after. She had started talking already. I've got one of my boys down there and he's phoned in to say that she's giving enough information to send Foster away for a long, long time."

"It's a good break, Tom, It's what you've been wanting. Once you get Foster put away, we're not going to have anything to talk about anymore."

"Look, Johnny, how do you figure in all this. Maybe, you don't. I want to be sure."

"What makes you think I figure in it all? Did Gladys say anything about me?"

"Who's Gladys?"

"Foster's wife."

"Don't tell me you've been laying her too?"

"She may bring me into it, Tom. I don't know. It's hard to know what Gladys is going to do. She's plenty sore at me right now. I don't know what she might say."

"I had a funny feeling that you might be mixed up in this, Johnny. We haven't told any of the newspapers about Foster's wife yet. I thought maybe I'd better sift through the thing before we let the reporters get at her."

"What about Foster? Have you arrested him?"

"Not yet. The boys are out with a warrant for him now. We had to go ahead and seize the records, though. It was a good thing you tipped us off. Foster did move all that stuff. A couple of hours after you called, he loaded up a station wagon and brought the stuff into the city. We grabbed it as soon as headquarters phoned to tell us his wife had showed up there. Don't worry, though. This has got nothing to do with you. You're out of it. Foster will think his wife tipped us off about the records, too. I haven't had a chance to look at them yet."

"Look at them, Tom. There's enough there. Throw the book at him. The son-of-a-bitch has got it coming to him."

"What about this killing down there? Do you think that Foster is mixed up in it? Even if he is, I don't see how it will do us any good. It's damn hard to hang a murder rap on a guy when he's up here and the murder is down there. I spoke to Feinberg, the head of our Miami bureau and he says that police have had some of Foster's men in for questioning already and that they can't get any information out of them. Feinberg's got a personal theory that if Foster did engineer this killing he didn't use any of his regular boys. Feinberg thinks that Foster probably hired some special talent to go down there and do the job."

"It could be me, huh?"

"It could look that way, Johnny. You know how they build up circumstantial evidence, Foster has been doing a lot of long distance telephoning to Miami today and tonight. I know that they are tracing all the calls. You spoke to him, didn't you?"

"Yes. A couple of times."

"Well, someone will be around to ask you questions. Have you got the answers? You fit Feinberg's theory pretty well. He's a good man, Feinberg, but when he gets an idea, he's pretty determined. If he thinks Foster sent down an outside man, you're going to have to have an awfully good story to convince him that it's not you."

"I've been in my room all night. Foster has had two men guarding my door. I couldn't have gotten out if I wanted to."

"How come Foster has been guarding your door?"

"It's a long story, Tom. He's been trying to keep me away from some people down here. Anyway, his watchdogs can testify that I haven't left the room."

"Johnny, don't misunderstand me. I'm on your side. Remember that. But there are going to be a couple of things which don't hang together. I tried to call you before, earlier, as soon as the news came through about Foster's wife. Nobody answered the phone, Johnny."

"I was sleeping. Foster called too. I slept through a couple of phone calls."

"O.K., Johnny."

"Tom, this is the straight stuff. I didn't kill Penicke. Maybe I know more about it than I should, but I didn't kill him. If they ask me any questions, Tom, I'm not going to talk. I'm sorry but I won't. I know that I may be interfering with justice and all that, but I won't talk."

"No dame can be worth that much."

"I didn't say anything about a dame, did I?"

"I said that I was on your side, Johnny."

"For your own good, Tom, forget you know me. Let them go ahead with their investigation. I'll come out all right. Forget you ever knew me. Play dumb."

"I'm only trying to help."

"I know that. I appreciate it. But you can't help, Tom. Just believe me when I tell you that I didn't kill anybody."

"I believe you. But you're going to be in the middle of a lot of circumstances. Are you sure you can get out all right?"

"I'll get out all right."

"O.K., boy. I tried. I'd hate to see anything bad happen to you. It would give the old neighborhood a bad reputation."

"If anything important breaks and you can do it without getting yourself in trouble, call me, will you? Reverse the charges if you want to."

"I don't have to reverse the charges. This is all being done on the taxpayers' dough."

"Thanks for trying to help, Tom. One good thing has happened anyway. You've got Foster where you want him."

"We've got Foster, all right. I hope we don't end up having you, too."

"So long, Tom,"

There wasn't much time, I would have to move quickly. I was sure now that I couldn't stay out of it, that Shirley and I would be drawn into the mess. It would take a lot of explaining. Once the truth was out, I felt that it would be the end of living for me.

The only thing I could think of was escape. I would escape with her and we would be together until they found us. I didn't have illusions about escaping forever. I knew that no matter where we went, they would find us. But I wanted to have her all to myself, I wanted to live as much of a lifetime as I could with her. Even if it would be for only two or three days. Whatever time there was left, I wanted to have with her.

I looked at my watch. It was fifteen minutes until midnight. She wouldn't be through at the Flamingo for another three-quarters of an hour. Time was running short.

I picked up the phone. "This is Mr. Maguire in room 816. I'm expecting a long distance call," I said, "I have to go out. Will you tell them to call back in three hours? I'll be back here at three o'clock this morning."

"All right, Mr. Maguire."

"If anyone else comes on the switchboard, be sure that they get that message, will you?"

"Yes, sir."

If the police came around to look for me, that would stall them for a few hours anyway. It would give us a head start and I hoped enough time to find a place to hide out.

O.K., so I was acting like a jerk. I wasn't using my head. I know all that. But I knew too that once they found us, we would never be together again. I would have the rest of my life to live with an unsated hunger for her. Years of famine. I wanted to store up a lot of loving in the time we had left, as much as I could to last me through the years of not having her. Maybe it doesn't make sense to some guys. If it doesn't, then those guys don't know what it is to love. Feel sorry for them, not me.

Because I knew that we would be caught eventually, I had no more fear. The two bird dogs in the hall had left. I walked right into the Flamingo and took a table and listened to her sing. She was really good. During her second number, she spotted me in the audience. Her forehead wrinkled in a frown. I smiled and blew her a kiss. She understood that everything was under control and from then on she sang right at me.

It was a good audience that night. I guess they all knew what had happened at the club and they were all nerves and excitement. She captured all that nervousness and held them still while she sang. She had the kind of voice that comes right up and sits on your lap, whispers in your ear, blows on the back of your neck and nibbles at your chin.

They kept her on for a long time. When the m.c. finally broke up the applause and introduced the next act, I ducked out and went back to her dressing room. The door was open. She was in there and the pansy piano player was talking. "You were simply devastating," he was saying. "You were a dream. I can't tell you how simply marvelous you sounded, Sandra. New York will be after us now. New York and bright lights. Your name in lights."

He didn't know that I was standing behind him, Shirley had seen me and was looking at me all the time the piano player was talking. There might have been those things for her, big-time singing engagements. Movies. She sure as hell had what it takes. There might have been big things for her if it hadn't been for me. This was the new life she was going to lead. All the things the piano player was telling her might have been a part of it. But her eyes were telling me that she didn't want it. They were saying that all she wanted was me. None of these other things mattered any more.

She got rid of the piano player and as soon as we were alone, we were in each other's arms. "Darling," she said, "it's going to be all right, isn't it? They don't suspect anything, do they?"

"It's all right. But we're going away. Now."

"Why?"

"I'll tell you later. Let's go."

"Something is wrong. You wouldn't be running away unless something is wrong."

"I told you that it's going to be all right. But let's get moving."

"All right, Johnny. We'll go back to my hotel and I'll pack."

"There isn't time. We'll buy what we need when we get where we're going."

"Where are we going?"

"I don't know yet. We'll see. Come on."

She took off her evening dress and started to put on the dress she had worn in the afternoon. "I have money when we need it, Johnny. You know that."

"O.K. We'll see what happens."

We walked a block down from the Flamingo, then got into a cab and drove out to the airport. I checked to see what flights were going out at that time. There were two scheduled within a half hour. I called Shirley over. "Where do you want to go, Kitten, New Orleans or Atlanta?"

"I don't care, Johnny. Wherever you say. Wherever we'll be safe."

I bought two tickets to New Orleans. While we were waiting to get on the plane, I went to the newsstand and looked through the papers. The later editions had no further news on Penicke's killing. The headlines were still thick and heavy. There were a lot of pictures, pictures of Penicke, the Flamingo and Penicke's girlfriend. There was nothing about Foster yet or about Gladys. The last paragraph in the Herald said, "Police have found no clues but are investigating all persons believed to have motives for the killing."

It was cold on the plane. Shirley was wearing only a thin dress and a very light-weight coat. I wore no top coat at all. We huddled close to each other in our seats and made the whole trip without talking very much. We were both tired and beat.

The plane was following a milk route. The trip took almost five hours. We landed several times but neither of us felt like getting out of the plane. I should have gotten out to see if the newspapers were carrying any new information but I decided I'd better stay with Shirley. There would be time in New Orleans to find out what was going on.

We arrived at five o'clock in the morning, New Orleans time. I went right to the newsstand. The morning paper carried the story on the front page but there were no new developments.

The only hotel I knew about in New Orleans was the Roosevelt. I figured there might be some questions if we tried to get in there without any luggage. There were some other hotels right on the fringe of the French Quarter. I asked the cab driver if he knew any of them. He rattled off a string of names. I asked him which one was the smallest. He said that the Chateau Blaine was the best of the small hotels. I told him to take us there.

The desk clerk was sleepy and looked at us with annoyance rather than surprise or suspicion. I registered as Mr. and Mrs. Christopher Weston. I smiled when I did it. Poor Tina, I was thinking. It was the first time that I had thought about Tina since I had left Chicago. Poor Tina. I had given her some bad times.

It wasn't too crummy a room for a third rate hotel. The bed sure as hell looked good to us. Believe it or not, we went right to sleep. There was no question of anything else. We went right to sleep huddled together as we had been on the plane and I don't think either of us changed position all the time we slept. We slept for about six hours. It was eleven in the morning when we woke up.

I called the desk and told them to send up the newspapers right away. I ordered breakfast from room service. Room service at the Chateau Blaine was a much different operation from the hotel in Miami. A man named Charley took our order over the phone, cooked the food and brought it up himself.

Shirley hadn't been out of bed all the time I was telephoning. She lay with her eyes opened in an empty stare. She hadn't asked any questions. She knew that there was a lot more wrong than I had told her. When the papers came up, I offered one to her but she shook her head. I couldn't blame her. It would have been swell not to know anything about anything.

The Penicke story was on the third page. Nothing new had broken. The story about Foster was still being held up for some reason. I couldn't understand that. Foster was a pretty big fish to fry. The papers would give it their deluxe treatment once they got hold of it. While I was reading, she said, "All right, Johnny?"

I smiled over to her. "So far, Kitten. I'll check the other paper." The other paper carried the same story. Still nothing new. "O.K.," I said. "It looks all right for a while."

She got out of bed, came over and sat on my lap. She nestled her head under my chin and snuggled close to me.

"You feel all right?" I said.

She nodded. "You?"

"I'm fine. You know what I feel like?"

"I want to eat breakfast first."

I laughed. "O.K. First we'll eat breakfast. Then we'll do what you want to do. Then we'll do what I want to do."

"Don't you want to do what I want to do?"

"Are you kidding? Sure, I do. But after that, I've got another idea."

"What?"

"I want to get married. To you."

She looked up at me. There were the beginnings of tears in her eyes, but she bit her lip and held them back.

"You're not going to start to cry? I'm proposing to you."

"It's bad, isn't it, Johnny? They're going to catch us."

"That's a hell of a way to talk. I'm proposing to you, Kitten. How can you talk about getting caught?"

"It's got something to do with it, hasn't it? If we get married, you won't have to tell them anything about me, will you? That's why you want to get married."

"That's only part of it," I said.

"It's not part of it, Johnny. It's all of it. I'm not fooling myself. You would never have married me if nothing had happened. You know that. Let's not pretend, Johnny. Let's not spoil anything by pretending. People like us don't get married."

"Look. I'm the only one who knows that you killed Penicke. If I'm your husband, they can't force me to testify against you. They can't make me tell what I know. The law says that I can refuse to say anything."

"But what about you, Johnny? Forget the law. Do you think you'll hold back information? Do you think you won't want to tell them what happened? Being married won't make any difference. You'll have to tell them. You're that kind of guy."

"All right. Forget it."

"How long have we got?"

"I don't know. It all depends how fast they find things out. However long it is, well be together. That's all that counts."

"Always, Johnny. Always."

While I was kissing her there was a knock on the door. It was the waiter with our breakfast. He put the tray down on the desk and then sat on the bed and started talking. It was really kind of funny. He was being very hospitable and telling us about his family and what a wonderful hotel this had been fifty years ago. We finally got rid of him and I finished kissing Shirley. Knowing that we would be caught had affected her deeply. It sharpened her desires and she clutched eagerly at me.

I said, "How about reversing the order of things around here? How about doing what you want to do before we eat breakfast?"

"The coffee will get cold."

"I don't give a damn."

"Nothing tastes worse than cold scrambled eggs." Her lips were right against mine while she was talking. She didn't give a damn about breakfast either. The only thing we gave a damn about was having each other.

# CHAPTER EIGHTEEN

It wasn't good. There was a strong, restless kind of hunger in both of us. Yet it wasn't good. Our doom hung over us, a heavy film of doom dulling our senses and dulling our pleasures. We struggled violently to find the terrific release we had known with each other. The struggle made our desires and cravings even stronger, building up the pitch of our love. But the release would not come. We pretended that the old excitement was there. We both pretended and knew that the other was pretending, too.

It ended without ending, and the dissatisfaction of it stayed in the room as a third person.

We ate the cold breakfast silently, looking out the window, down on to the long narrow street below. A sliver of sunshine had managed to penetrate through the close buildings. It was a nice day, warm with sunshine. "What do you want to do?" I asked.

"I don't care. It doesn't make any difference. What's the difference what we do?"

"More coffee?"

"No," she said, "it's cold. We should have eaten while the food was still hot."

"I'm sorry."

She didn't say anything for a few minutes. "I suppose I ought to buy some clothes. I can't wear this dress here, it's not warm enough."

"I suppose I ought to buy some clothes too. I need some shirts and underwear."

"Have you got any money left?"

I didn't answer. I was getting pretty low but I had enough to manage for a while. She got up to get her purse. She divided the roll of bills in half and threw one of the stacks on the table in front of me. I left it there. I was going to need it after a while but I couldn't touch it. "We haven't got much time," she said. "We might as well enjoy something while we can."

"I said I was sorry. You don't have to keep harping on it."

"I'm not harping on it. I only said that we might as well enjoy something."

"You know damn well that I wouldn't touch any of that money."

"Then don't touch it. I don't give a damn what you do."

She walked around the room for a while, restlessly, looking through the empty drawers and into the empty closet. She turned back to me. "Are you going to take a shower?"

I nodded that I was. "You go ahead first if you want to."

"I'm sorry, Johnny."

"What are you sorry about?"

"It was my fault. It wasn't yours. I was trying too hard. I wanted you too much. I was. . . . I don't know what was the matter."

She was my old girl again, the hardness and the bitterness was beginning to melt. I wanted to go to her and take her in my arms but I figured I had better not touch her. "We'll be all right." I said. "It was just this time. We were nervous and tired. We were too tied up."

"Won't we always be, Johnny, until they find us? Won't we always be tied up in knots?"

"Take a shower. You'll feel better."

"I wish it were that easy. It's not. It keeps eating at me."

"It's not easy for me either but I tell you it will be all right. The next time will be all right."

"It had better be."

"Or what? Are you threatening me? What if it isn't? Are you going out on the street and pick up the first pair of pants that comes along?"

"Johnny!" Her voice was pleading.

"Well, go ahead, I'm not going to stop you. Go ahead, go on out in the street."

"Johnny, don't. Don't talk like that. Don't let this happen to us."

I was all choked up inside. I couldn't talk any more. I didn't know whether I was going to start blubbering like a kid or throw the damn lamp through the window. She was waiting for me to say something else but I didn't.

"I'm going to take a shower, Johnny." Once more she waited for me to say something. Then she turned around and went into the bathroom, locking the door.

All the time she was in the shower, I looked at that wad of bills in front of me and remembered the poor bastard who had spent his whole life working to make it. I knew all the sweat and heartaches that that roll of bills meant. Then, bang, she tosses it in front of me. Just like that. What was that supposed to make me?

There are lots of names, I guess, for the thing which I felt that I was. Besides the legal name there was the word gigolo. Or pimp. In a way I was feeling like that.

Actually, I couldn't blame the girl. It wasn't Shirley's fault. The blame was mine. I should have never told her anything about Foster and Penicke. I should have never told her that I was in a jam. There was no way in which I could have known about her, known what she would do. There was no way for me to know that she was capable of killing. Yet it was not her crime, it was my crime. She had done the job that I should have done. And the guilt lay with me. I couldn't condemn her for that.

Yet I was condemning her. I was hearing the sound of the shower and seeing how she would look, the loveliness of her body, the softness and tightness of it. The stories she had told me about herself came back into my mind. There was the kitten which she had been to me. And there was the cat, the wild, clawing animal that she could also be. There was the destructive thing which she had been to Sam and to the soldier and to the man with the bullet in his stomach. I had a taste of that now. For the first time the kitten had shown its claws.

I did not like it.

She was in the shower a long time. It was a long time for thinking. I was thinking that in a very real sense, I was married to her. No matter what happened now, I wouldn't be able to leave her. No matter how she scratched at me and how she tried to tear me apart, I couldn't leave her. I had lost that independence, the independence which I had always had, the independence which left me free to say, "The hell with you, baby."

It was more than a marriage is, more binding than a marriage is. There could be no divorce. I could not divorce my conscience from my body. Her guilt was my guilt. Our lives were so constructed now that it could be no other way.

On the street below, there were people hurrying to somewhere and people strolling to nowhere. There were people laughing and people walking with determination, stern expressions on their faces.

There would be none of those things for us. There would be no use in hurrying or not hurrying. We would only have to wait, spend long hours waiting for the thing which would inevitably be coming.

The waiting was going to drive me nuts.

I don't remember how many names I called myself during the time she was in the shower. I had become everything I hated in other men. I was weak. No guts. A man without direction and, if my performance a little while before was any indication, I wasn't a hell of a man at all. Everything I had heard in school, all the talk about law and the spirit of the law, came back to me. I remembered the man I had been when I had finally come out of the Army. I had been full of fight and full of ambition. I had a direction to take and I was going to take it. I was going to be the hottest lawyer this side of the Rockies. More than that. Being a lawyer was going to mean something, it was going to be symbolic of my whole life.

The law was going to be a crusade with me. The law was a bright shining star somewhere, almost within my reach. I worked like hell to reach that star.

Kid stuff. Sure, it was kid stuff. Some of it had been rubbed off in law school and the rest of it had come off the hard way when I had tried to make a living by being a lawyer. The bright star was made of tin and the law was like any other business, a fight for sustenance, a survival of the fittest or the survival of the guy who knew his way around the right people.

Now that I was on the other side of the law, hiding in a dingy hotel in the French Quarter, the star was shining again. Right up there on the dirty, cracked ceiling, it was shining brightly. Maybe this one was made of tin, too. I didn't know. It didn't make any difference. A man does what he had to do. I had to reach for that star.

Shirley came out of the bathroom wrapped in a big towel. "Go ahead," she said. "You can go in there now. The water isn't very hot but what can you expect from a third rate hotel?"

"Come here, Kitten."

"I'm going to get dressed. I don't want to stay in this room any more than I have to. I feel as though I can't breathe."

"Listen to me for a minute. I've been doing some thinking."

"About what?"

"About what you said to me on the beach when I took you away," I said. "I was thinking about all the reasons you gave me for not running away with me. You were right. I should have believed you."

"It's too late now. You should have left it the way it was. You should have left me alone when I told you to. I had courage then. I thought I had done a big thing, made a big sacrifice. A great, big, beautiful gesture."

"It was," I said. "It took guts to do what you did."

"If you had had any guts you would have understood, you would have left me alone. You would have seen what it meant to me. You had changed me from something which I was and hated being into a woman in love. I was honest with you. I told you the truth about myself. If you had let me go through with this in my own way, I would have stayed like that. I would have stayed being a woman in love. I was the kind of person I had always wanted to be. It was my chance to prove to myself that I was something more than a good bed friend. ... Don't flinch, Johnny. Don't act so surprised. What else do you think there is between us now? Maybe it could have been more. But when you get right down to it, this wound up like everything else has always ended for me. It had a chance of being different. You spoiled that."

"I know that now," I said. "I understand that."

"It's a fine time. What are you driving at? Do you think you can ditch me now? If you think that, you're wrong. You're not tossing me over and letting me land in the hands of the cops."

"I didn't say that I was. You're going to be all right," I said. "I'm going to give myself up. I'm going to confess."

"What are you talking about?"

"I'm going to the police and tell them that I did it. They'll believe me."

"What about me? What am I supposed to do? Am I supposed to stand by and watch while they put your head in a noose?"

"You don't have to come into it at all. You can take off. You've got dough. You can sing. You wanted a career, didn't you? If you want, I can say that I did this for love. I can say that I killed for love. You'll get your picture in the paper that way. Every blood-thirsty bastard in the country will know what you look like. You'll have offers from every night club in business. You'll be famous."

"That's just swell. That's just fine. How bad do you think I am? I've got something decent in me. Maybe not much, but enough to know that I couldn't let you take the blame for something which I did."

"I'm to blame for this. I would have killed him if you hadn't. That's why I got out of my room. I got out to kill Penicke. You got there first. That doesn't change the fact that you did it for me. It was my job and you did it."

"That's a good story but there's one hitch," she said. "I still held the gun when it went off."

"If you keep your mouth shut, nobody will know."

"Am I supposed to keep my ..." Suddenly she stopped and a change came over her again. "Johnny, Johnny, what are we doing? What are we saying to each other?" She ran to me and buried her face in my lap. "I love you. I didn't mean to say those things. I love you. Let's not give up. Let's take what time there is and live, Johnny. Don't let me spoil our love. Don't let me."

"It's no use, Kitten. It's no use. You know it and I know it. It doesn't change our love. It doesn't change the last two days. We'll always have that."

"I wish I had my courage back, Johnny. I wish I had the courage to do what I want to do. I'd get you out of it then. I'd tell the truth. But I'm scared. All the way down inside, I'm scared."

I put my arm around her and held her tightly. "I'm not scared, Kitten. I'll have courage enough for both of us."

"What are you going to do?"

"Promise me one thing. Promise me that you'll never tell anyone that you killed Penicke."

"I won't promise. Johnny, I won't. I won't let them hurt you for something you didn't do."

"Don't you see that if they took you away from me, there would be nothing for me anyway? I'm the guilty one. In my heart, I know it."

"I won't, Johnny. I won't."

"I was wrong in Miami. I stopped you from doing something which was important. I was wrong to do that. It was selfish. Don't you make the mistake that I made. This is important for me.

Please, don't make the mistake that I made. I'm going to do what I wouldn't let you do."

I lifted her head from my lap. She fell to the floor and stayed there crying. I went to the telephone and put through a call to Tom White. The circuits to Chicago were busy and I lighted a cigarette and lay on the bed waiting for the call to go through. She didn't move from the floor. In five minutes the call came through and I heard Tom's excited voice. "For Christ's sake, Maguire, where the hell are you?"

"New Orleans, Tom. I ran away. I'm sorry."

"I've been trying to reach you in Miami. I've got good news. The heat's off."

"What do you mean, the heat's off?"

"You're not going to get mixed up in this. I worked it out so your name won't even come up."

"I am mixed up in it though. All the way up to my neck."

"But you're not, Johnny. Holy cow, I've been working all night on this thing. The only thing anybody knows about you is that you spoke to Foster a couple of times last night. Feinberg was suspicious but I got to him before he did anything. I told him that you were a friend of ours here, that you had been working with us on the Foster case. I told him that you were the man who had given us the tip about Foster moving all his records."

"You shouldn't have done that, Tom. I told you to forget that you ever knew me."

"Why not? It's all true, isn't it? Everything I told him was true."

"But I am mixed up in it, Tom."

"But you said that you didn't kill him. That's the important thing. You said that you didn't kill him. I believed you. I wasn't wrong, was I?"

I hesitated a minute. "No, Tom, you weren't wrong. I didn't kill him."

"O.K., so then why should you get involved in it?"

"There's something you ought to know."

"Don't tell me, Johnny. I don't want to know anything else. I know as much as I want."

"Are you sure?"

"Of course, I'm sure. Listen, Johnny, you're a hero up here. You gave us the tip on Foster. Of course, nobody knows that but me and the chief and Feinberg down in Miami."

"Did you get Foster? Have you arrested him?"

"We got him all right. He's all ready to croak his wife. What he called her! One of his other lawyers sprung him right away. He's out on bail but it doesn't make any difference. This time we've got him for sure."

"What about his wife? How much talking has she done?"

"I went down to see her early this morning. There was a line in her confession about you, nothing important. Something about your being mad at her husband. I dropped a hint down there that you were a special agent or something and that we'd just as soon your name wasn't connected with this in any way. It worked fine. They crossed the part about you right out of the confession. It won't come up in the trial, either. We're working out all of Mrs. Foster's testimony. Don't worry, you won't figure in it."

"What about Foster? He thinks I did the killing."

"It doesn't make any difference. Foster isn't even being questioned about the murder down there. We know that we don't have a chance. He won't say anything. When he goes to court, it will be on income tax evasion. He won't be talking about anything else."

"You're quite a guy, Tom. I owe you a beer for this."

"You don't owe me anything, Johnny. I owe you a whole bottle of champagne. I'm the fair-haired boy around here today. Don't forget I'm the one who got the information about the records being moved. Without those records, we couldn't make our case stick. The chief thinks I'm a pretty hot operator. You don't owe me anything, my boy."

"I'm still going to buy you a beer."

"Are you coming right back here?"

"I don't know yet. I have a few things to figure out first."

"I'm going home right now and get some sleep. Even if it means muzzling my kids, I'm going home and sleep until tomorrow morning. Incidentally, Johnny, how's the girl friend?"

"Fine," I said. "Just fine."

"I can hardly wait to hear about it."

"O.K."

"I know you, Maguire, you're the kind who never talks about anything like that. I'll keep asking anyway."

"Goodbye, Tom. And thanks."

"Take care of yourself. Call me when you get back."

When I turned from the phone, I saw that Shirley had stopped crying and was sitting up on the floor.

"What happened? What did he say?"

"We're out of it. Tom has kept my name out of it. We won't be mixed up in it."

"Who is Tom?"

"Tom is an old friend of mine. He knows all about this case. He's managed to keep us clear. Penicke's murder will go unsolved. I guess the police don't care much. They're glad to have a guy like him out of the way."

She stood up. "You mean that we're free? No one is looking for us? No one is going to bother us?"

"No one will bother us. We can go out and not worry."

She tightened the towel around her body. "Now what?" she asked.

"You tell me," I said. "Now what?"

"I don't know. I almost wish it hadn't happened this way. It's going to seem so funny to be free. Not right. And nothing will be different for me, I'll end up being the same as I always was. I've lost my chance to be anything different."

"Whatever you want to do," I said. "I'll do whatever you want."

She laughed, hard and bitterly. "That's just swell. Whatever I want you to do, huh? Do we have to stay together just because we've been through this? Are we going to have to spend our whole lives hating each other just because we have a murder in common?"

"You don't hate me. I don't hate you."

"It's not going to be any good for us, Johnny. You know that."

"We ought to take that chance."

"I don't think so. I don't think we've got a chance."

"So what happens?"

"You go your way and I go my way."

"Doesn't it make any difference that we love each other? Doesn't that matter to you?"

"The kind of love that you're talking about exists in the head. It's all in the mind. It's no good without the other kind of love. And we're not going to be good for each other anymore. I can tell. I know when it stops. You'll always be sleeping with a woman who murdered a man. And I'll be sleeping with a man who spoiled my one chance to be something decent."

"You're doing this purposely. You're trying to make yourself out something which you're not. You still believe in your jinx, don't you?"

"I don't know what I believe. I only know that we had something wonderful and that we don't have it any more. If we go on together, we'll spoil even the memory of it. That's important to me."

"What will you do?"

"Go back to Miami. I'll see if my job at the Flamingo is still there. If it's not, I'll find another job. There's the money. I've got a lot of it to see me through."

I pointed to the desk where I had been sitting. The roll of bills lay there next to the half-eaten eggs. "Don't forget that," I said.

"What are you going to do, Maguire?"

"Go back, I guess. Pick up where I left off. Maybe I'll have some new steam when I get back. I think that I'll want to do more than I've been doing."

"You'd better take a shower while the water is still hot. I want to get dressed."

"I guess, maybe, I should."

I went to her and took her in my arms and kissed her. There was a flash of the old fire. I felt it and she felt it. "Don't, Johnny," she whispered. "Let it go at this. It's better this way. I know what I'm doing."

I went into the bathroom and stood in front of the mirror for a couple of minutes. I looked at my face. There was nothing to see, only blankness and unshaved emptiness. I was beyond the point of feeling. There had been so much in my life, so much which had come so quickly. Then gone.

As I was looking into the mirror, I saw the door knob turning behind me. The door opened a crack and then it didn't open any more. I waited. Then the door opened quickly and she walked in saying my name, "Johnny!" It was more than saying my name. She was saying a whole lot of things, all the things which there were between us. She was saying what we had been to each other and she was saying the love which was unfinished in our lives.

But when I turned to her, she stopped. Whatever words she had ready to say, she didn't say them. She bit her lip to hold them back. But her eyes said them as clearly as if her lips had spoken them. I had to hold on to the sink to keep from going to her. If she had the strength to hold back the words, I would have to have the strength to hold back my body. Once before I had messed her up. I had stopped her from doing the thing which it was so important for her to do. I wasn't going to do that again. This was going to be the way she wanted it.

It took a few moments before she regained control of herself. "I thought I left my comb in here," she said. "Is it on the sink?"

I shook my head. "I think maybe it's on the dresser."

She forced some laughter. "It probably is. I thought I left it in here, but now I think I remember seeing it on the dresser."

"Kitten, if you want to . . . ."

She wouldn't let me finish. "That's right, I did leave it on the dresser. I don't know what made me think it was in here." She walked out of the bathroom and closed the door. From the sound of her voice I knew that she was close to tears. But this was going to be her way. This was going to be the way she wanted it to be. It took all the strength I had to keep from following her through that door.

The water was still fairly hot. I stayed in the shower for a long time. When I came out, she was gone. I had known that she would be. It was what she had wanted, the way she had wanted it to be.

I dressed slowly, went down to pay the hotel bill and then walked out into the street. I walked with the crowds of people, let myself be caught in the current of their movement and became lost in them.

# CHAPTER NINETEEN

The next days were lost days. Days in which darkness and light were continuously blended into one and there was no day and there was no night, there was only a blur of grayness. There were hours of consciousness and there were hours of unconsciousness, and these not clearly defined. Wake seeming as sleep and sleep sometimes as vivid as consciousness.

New Orleans is a good town to be lost in. It's not very clear to me what I did or where I went. Once the crowd picked me up in its pattern, my memory blanks out except for occasional images of bars and tawdry rooms, narrow streets and dark alleys. I don't know where I was and I don't know who I was with. Maybe in many places and with many people.

I remember waking up. I woke up in an apartment. A small, dingy apartment-filled with china dogs and cats, layers of curtains over the windows and dusty jalousies screening off the light. There was no one in the apartment. The bed I woke up in had dirty sheets and looked as though it hadn't been made in a month. I had reached that point in a drunk where I was immune to liquor, nothing more I would drink would have any effect.

It was hot in the room. Hot and stuffy. Hard to breathe in. I got out of bed and tried to get through the layers of curtains to open the window. Dust came out like clouds of smoke. I began to cough and as soon as I coughed I knew just how bad a shape I was in. In desperation I pulled and the whole drapery came down. I pushed back the jalousies and threw open the window.

There was light in the room now. I walked to the mirror over the dresser and looked at myself. I was thinner and there were bruises on the side of my head. There was a wound on my lip which had healed. The crust of the scab was big and ugly.

I was wearing the same pair of shorts I had been wearing when I left Miami. They were dirty and ripped. My clothes were in a heap on the floor. I was in great condition.

What I wanted most was a bath. I couldn't find the bathroom. There was a sitting room and a bedroom in the apartment. No bath. It was an old building so I figured there might be a community one in the hall. There was.

An old negro woman was out there sweeping. She looked at me and there was no expression in her face. The bathroom was big, lighted from a skylight. The tub was not clean. I washed it out as well as I could then let the hot water run while I went back to the apartment to look for a towel. I found one that was a little soiled and smelled of cheap perfume. It was better than nothing.

When I finally dressed, I looked like a bum but at least I was clean underneath the torn clothes and dirty shirt. I felt for my wallet. It was gone. I didn't have a scrap of identification and I didn't have any money. I tried to think of someone I might know in New Orleans but there wasn't anyone.

I took a chance and searched through the dresser drawers. They were filled with a woman's paraphernalia, cheap, brightly colored stuff all smelling of the same perfume. Under the lining of one of the drawers, I found sixty dollars. I stuffed the money in my pocket, got out of the apartment in a hurry and ran down the four flights of stairs.

When I was on the street, I thought about Shirley for the first time. There was a picture of her in my mind. It was a picture that I knew I would be carrying for a long time. I walked a couple of blocks, found a cab and headed for the railroad station. I bought a couple of papers and searched through them for any news about

Foster or Penicke. There was nothing. Five days had gone by and there were new murders and there was new excitement.

The train left at five o'clock and I was in Chicago the next morning at nine-thirty.

There was a stack of mail waiting for me which I ran through quickly at the desk in the lobby of my apartment building. They were mostly bills and ads. There was one envelope postmarked Los Angeles with a woman's hand writing on it. I opened it quickly but it was from someone I had gotten a divorce for a year ago, who had remarried and was living in California. She wanted to know about California divorce laws now. She married the wrong man again.

There were some phone messages. Two from Tom White, which had "nothing important" written across the bottom. There was a call from a Lt. Stanleigh at Police Headquarters. The message was dated two days ago. He was the man who had awakened me that morning so long ago to tell me that Shirley had committed suicide. The other telephone message was from my laundry. I think my bill was overdue.

I called Stanleigh as soon as I got upstairs.

"I've been trying to get hold of you, Mr. Maguire."

"I've been out of town. What's up?"

"I thought you'd like to know that your girlfriend has turned up."

"What are you talking about?"

"Mrs. Wolffner. We found her body a couple of days ago. It was washed up on the beach not far from where she used to live."

I shouldn't have been surprised. But it hit me all over again, right between the eyes. It was for keeps this time. This is what she had wanted. I knew that.

Stanleigh's voice started again. He sounded so God damn pleasant. "What's the matter, Maguire, so choked up you can't say anything?"

"What kind of condition was the body in?"

"Beautifully preserved," he said. "The ice, you know. It's just like a deep freeze. Quite a looker, wasn't she, Maguire? Can't say that I blame you. We're holding the body. We can't find any relatives but I told them down at the morgue to hold her until I got in touch with you. I suppose she don't look so good any more. But you can go down there and see her if you want to. You know where the morgue is? It's in the County Building. You can go down there to claim the body. I'll tell them it's all right."

"What happens if I don't claim her?"

"We'll bury her in the city yard."

"Don't do that. I'll have the body taken care of."

"Do you want me to tell them you'll be down?"

"I won't come myself. I'll send someone for her. An undertaker."

"There's a release that will have to be signed."

"I'll have that taken care of," I said.

"Okey dokey, Maguire. Just as long as you take care of it. They don't like to keep bodies this long but I knew that you had a personal interest."

"Thanks, very much."

I looked through the classified directory and picked out an undertaker that advertised a crematory service. I arranged for them to pick up the body at the morgue and cremate it. and throw the ashes back into the lake. That was all that there was for me to do.

She would be gone then. Nothing left of her except pictures in my mind—memories hidden in corners of my consciousness and subconsciousness. I had nothing left and yet there was a lot which I would be remembering. There would be a lump in my throat, an insatiable hunger in the pit of my stomach. I would see a girl and the way this girl would have of moving her hands or glancing over her shoulder would remind me of Shirley. I would hear a song, one of the songs which she had sung and she would be with me again. I would see a kitten playing and remember the days which we had had together.

Words of prayers I had said when I was a kid came back to me. Fragments of Latin incantations ran through my head. All the words seemed to be having meaning now. Words that had been words to a kid were words with meaning. They were words which were meant for me and for the thing which I was feeling.

I picked up the phone and called Tina at her office. When she heard my voice, she said my name, "Johnny." The sounding of the name caught all the fear which she had been feeling. Then she said it again. "Johnny." This time I could hear the relief from fear. "Are you all right? I've been out of my mind worrying about you. Where were you? Where have you been?"

"I had to go out of town on business," I said. "A client of mine wanted me to look at some property in Florida. I meant to drop you a note but I was so damn busy that I didn't get a chance. I was wondering what you're doing tonight. I thought maybe you'd come over and cook some dinner for me."

What the hell. A guy has got to go on living.

Made in the USA
Monee, IL
25 January 2021